"Why are yo

"Whatever you felt ___ continued. "And y___ ___ ___ ___ never looked at you that way." She bit the inside of her cheek after telling the half lie.

"You're right on one point," Cade said. "I still care for you, Reno. But I don't ever want to hurt you again. I'll be going back to Idaho after Dad—"

She gave a dry laugh. "Cade, everyone I've ever cared about has left me in one way or another. I'm afraid I don't trust anyone anymore. So you see, you're here preaching to the choir." She held out her hands, palms up. "I've already told myself I'll never let you hurt me again. I feel nothing for you, Cade. Not contempt, not love…nothing."

Liar.

She could forgive him for leaving her, but she couldn't forget.

Dear Reader,

This book is very dear to my heart, as Reno is a woman much like me. Proud of her American Indian heritage, Reno Blackwell loves the land, especially the mountains of Colorado. She does her best to live in harmony with the wild mustangs that roam her ranch and the government property surrounding it. In honor of her grandfather's memory, Reno has created a sanctuary for those mustangs too old, lame or otherwise unwanted for adoption.

Like the horses she loves, Reno's had a tough row to hoe—betrayed by the man she thought of as her father, left alone when her grandfather passed away. And deserted by Cade Lantana, a good-looking cowboy seven years her senior.

Reno hung on to the courage she'd learned from Grandpa Mel and stayed at her home in Eagle's Nest, on Wild Horse Ranch, where she created the mustang sanctuary. But she's never forgotten the betrayal she felt when Cade left Eagle's Nest. Now Cade is back, a BLM ranger, out to get the poachers who are stealing the mustangs Reno loves with all her heart.

Reno is also determined to see the poachers pay for their crimes, and equally determined to guard her heart against Cade.

Come with me, dear reader, and ride the trails of Colorado's western slope. Let's see what it takes for a strong-headed woman and an equally strong hero to forget the past and focus on the future.

I love hearing from my readers. You can reach me at BrendaMott@hotmail.com. Please reference the book title on the subject line.

Brenda Mott

COWBOY FOR KEEPS
Brenda Mott

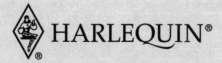

HARLEQUIN®

TORONTO • NEW YORK • LONDON
AMSTERDAM • PARIS • SYDNEY • HAMBURG
STOCKHOLM • ATHENS • TOKYO • MILAN • MADRID
PRAGUE • WARSAW • BUDAPEST • AUCKLAND

ISBN-13: 978-0-373-71526-8
ISBN-10:   0-373-71526-9

COWBOY FOR KEEPS

ABOUT THE AUTHOR

When Brenda Mott isn't busy writing or rescuing animals—she has more than thirty dogs at any given time—she enjoys curling up with a good book (naturally!), riding her horses or walking her dogs along the riverbank. Brenda can trace her family roots back to the Cherokees who walked the Trail of Tears, and her ranch—twenty-one acres deep in the Tennessee woods—is located on part of what used to be the original claims of the Cherokee Nation. Brenda's stories often reflect her love of horses by having a ranch-themed plot. She enjoys writing romance best of all, because there's always a guaranteed happy ending. She loves hearing from her readers. You may reach her at BrendaMott@hotmail.com.

Books by Brenda Mott

HARLEQUIN SUPERROMANCE

1037–SARAH'S LEGACY
1127–COWGIRL, SAY YES
1211–THE NEW BABY
1257–THE CHOSEN CHILD
1286–TO PROTECT HIS OWN
1369–MAN FROM MONTANA
1430–THE SHERIFF OF SAGE BEND

This book is dedicated to my father, his father and to my son, Chance *(a-da-na-ta di-ni-la-wi)* and my cousin, Melvyn—Cherokee men who are every bit as tough and loving as Reno's Grandpa Mel. And to my daughter, Loretta—a smart, strong woman like Reno. *Neh-go-he-luh ah-yuh-we-yah.*

CHAPTER ONE

LIGHTNING CUT ACROSS the sky with a vengeance, turning darkness to light for the span of a heartbeat. Long enough to give Reno Blackwell a clear glimpse of the horses. They raced through the clearing below, scattering like spilled marbles. Flared nostrils and urgent whinnies made their fear palpable—more so than the pounding of hooves on rock.

Without a second thought, Reno sent her own mount plunging over the edge of the hillside. The ground slid away beneath the blue roan, rock striking rock as Plenty Coups tucked his haunches and propelled himself forward in a hell-bent-for-leather descent.

Thunder rumbled like an angry spirit, and the long-awaited rain poured down relentlessly. As horse and rider reached the bottom of the slope, Reno searched the darkness for signs of human movement. She prayed for another flash of lightning, a glimpse of a headlight…anything to help her locate the poachers.

There. At the edge of the clearing.

All-terrain vehicles moved easily across the rocky ground, driving the mustangs forward, herding them along. Reno spotted at least two ATVs—and men with rifles—before the sky blackened again, but she could still see the bobbing glow of headlights. Her pulse pounded in her temples.

The mustangs. Her mustangs… At the sight of the men's rifles, she'd tasted the sharp copper of adrenaline, but now thoughts of her own safety fled. She had to turn the herd.

With a shout of rage, Reno dug her heels into her gelding's sides, rain rolling off the brim of her hat as she leaned forward in the saddle. If she could steer the mustangs away from the mouth of the canyon ahead, they might have a chance. Once inside, they would be trapped. In another flash of lightning—the bolt too close for comfort now—she spotted the Judas horse, one sent by the poachers to lure the mustangs onward. He was running ahead of the herd, showing them the way. She pointed the blue roan straight at him.

Plenty Coups responded like the warrior he was named for. Fearless and surefooted, he galloped along the sagebrush-dotted wash, despite the darkness. Like Reno, he'd been born on this land, and he stretched his neck out now, pinning his ears back as she leaned low in the saddle and urged him to run.

As they approached the Judas horse, a gray, Reno

pulled her sodden cowboy hat off and waved it, shouting. Her voice was mostly lost amid the noise of the running herd, the thunder and the roar of the ATVs, but the gray pricked his ears and rolled his eyes.

Rain soaked Reno's hair and got into her eyes, but the wind whipped it away. She shouted again, angling in tighter. The blue roan's hooves beat a steady rhythm, taking her closer.

Out of the corner of her eye, she caught a sudden movement. Another rider was racing through the sagebrush, silhouetted against the stormy sky. Reno had just enough time to wonder where on earth he'd come from before he reached her. His horse, dark as the night around them, sped past Plenty Coups, coming at the gray from the opposite side. As a team, they cut off the animal.

Reno saw a sudden flash, like light reflecting from a spur, as the cowboy on the dark horse turned the gray, and then the herd. Waving his arms, he sent them in an arc, while she rode behind him, backing his efforts. The shouted curses of the men on the ATVs was music to her ears, and Reno let out a whoop. Her grandfather, a full-blooded Apache, had also loved the mustangs, and she'd be damned if a group of money-grubbing poachers would ever touch one hair of their manes.

Not on her land.

A bullet whizzed past her ear, and for one heart-stopping moment, she thought the gray had been hit. But he raced on, blending with the herd. Turning in the saddle, Reno drew her pistol from the holster beneath her black oilskin and fired at the headlight of an ATV. The glass shattered, knocking out the bulb, and she shot again, hitting another. She heard curses, and one high-pitched scream that made her laugh.

Not so tough now, are you?

She'd been born in the saddle, according to her grandfather, with a pistol in one hand and a knife in the other. *Come closer, scumbags, and I'll show you an old Apache trick.*

But the poachers had had enough. Their ATVs roared around and sped back up through the canyon, the sound echoing off the walls as they retreated. Reno tugged on her reins, gradually slowing Plenty Coups, who shook his head. She knew he wanted to keep running with the herd—*his* herd once.

The wild horses swept away, disappearing like shadows into the night. The lightning seemed to follow them, creating one last light show across the expanse of Colorado sky before the storm rumbled to a subdued downpour.

But not before Reno saw him clearly.

In the last flash of lightning, the cowboy on the black horse sat still in the saddle, blending into the sagebrush. Reno felt the air leave her lungs as she realized why he'd seemed familiar.

She knew his face, all right. One that still haunted her sleep.

Cade Lantana.

The man who had stolen her heart.

Then killed her father.

RENO RODE HOME without looking back, her thoughts churning. Never in a million years would she have expected to run into Cade. He'd rattled her worse than the poachers had.

"Where the hell did you come from?" she'd demanded, and he'd laughed at her bluntness. But not with humor. Reno found nothing funny about his return to Eagle's Nest, either.

She cursed under her breath. That was all she needed—help from the man who'd abandoned her nine years ago, after she'd lost her parents. Sonny Sanchez had turned out to be scum, but he'd been the only father she'd ever known. And Reno had looked up to Cade as a big brother, until he'd left her when she needed him most.

It was close to midnight by the time she finished unsaddling Plenty Coups, rubbing him down and putting him in a warm stall with hay and fresh water. Exhausted, she headed for the house, which sat almost dead center on the two thousand acres of Wild Horse Ranch, not far from the barn. Grandpa Mel had liked being close to his horses, and Reno found comfort in it, too. In summer, she slept with her windows open and loved hearing the occasional whinny floating on the air like a lullaby.

As she walked up the four steps to the wide porch now, her dogs greeted her, tails wagging, bodies wriggling with excitement as though she'd been gone for days. Her German shepherds—one white, the other black-and-tan—towered over the two mutts she'd rescued. Two sweet dogs, unwanted, dropped off on a desolate mountain road near her ranch… It sickened Reno, the things people did to animals.

She petted all four, then opened the screen door and stepped into the mudroom. After kicking off her boots, she made her way through the living room and into the lighted kitchen.

"Wynonna, what are you doing up?" Reno thought she'd been quiet enough leaving the house to not disturb the housekeeper.

Wynonna studied her in the soft glow of the twin wrought-iron lamps, shaped like roosters, that hung on either side of the sink. A Lakota Sioux, she'd worked for Grandpa Melvern for more years than Reno could count, long before Reno had been born, and had stepped without question into the role of mother when Reno's own mom had overdosed. And Wynonna had stayed when the second of two strokes took Grandpa Mel's life.

"I heard you ride out a while ago. Want some hot

chocolate?" Without waiting for an answer, the older woman poured a mug for Reno, then sat cradling her own in both hands, her slippered feet propped on the vacant chair beside her. "Is it the horses?"

Reno nodded as she sipped the rich, sweet cocoa, feeling its warmth chase away the aftereffects of the storm, the danger. "I thought the poachers might try something, what with everybody busy in town." Independence Day, with a big parade, three-day rodeo and fireworks display, would keep Sheriff Pritchard and his deputies occupied through the weekend, rain or no.

"I knew it wasn't the possibility of canceled fireworks keeping you home," Wynonna said, her dark eyes knowing.

"You didn't really have a headache, either, did you?"

Wynonna's laugh lines deepened as she flipped her long, salt-and-pepper braid over her shoulder. "I wanted to be here in case you needed me," she admitted. "I also figured I might as well stay out of your way and let you look after your horses. But I did call Austin, since I was worried for your safety. He said he would come out if we needed him."

Reno nodded. Austin Pritchard had been sheriff of Garfield County for five years, a deputy before that, and he was good at his job, if a little too gung ho at times. He was an attractive-looking man, thirty-three years old, tall, blond…most women's idea of a catch. Plus he had a crush on Reno as wide as the Colorado River. Reno wasn't sure she was looking for a catch, but that hadn't stopped her from going out with the man.

Automatically, she found herself thinking of Cade, who'd also once been a deputy sheriff. Now *there* was a man who could turn heads, with his sun-streaked brown hair and blue-green eyes. But hell would freeze over before she'd let him back in her heart. "Did you know Cade Lantana is in town?"

Wynonna nearly missed the table edge as she set down her mug. "No, I didn't. Where did you hear that?"

"I ran into him tonight." Reno told her about the poachers and Cade, leaving out the part about being shot at. Wy tended to worry.

"I wondered if he would come back to help his mother," Wynonna said, "with his dad being so sick."

Matthew Lantana's emphysema had deteriorated to the point where he needed oxygen on a regular basis. That was a virtual death sentence to a rough-and-tumble cowboy. Estelle Lantana was having a hard time running their cattle operation, since the mounting medical expenses had forced her and Matt to let go most of their ranch hands.

"Cade's a man of honor," Wynonna added.

"Don't start." Reno knew the other woman had hoped, years ago, that Reno and Cade would some-day have a future together. But things had never been that way between them. At twenty-five, Cade had *still* viewed eighteen-year-old Reno as a kid, even though she could tell by the way he some-times looked at her that he thought she was pretty. His own looks hadn't escaped her, and she'd had a crush on him, for sure. But she'd longed so much for a big brother that she'd tried hard to impress him every chance she got. She'd wanted him to be proud of her.

Wynonna had read more into it. The seven-year age difference between Reno and Cade hadn't both-ered her the way it had Grandpa Mel. Or maybe it was just that Reno's grandfather had deemed no man good enough for his granddaughter, least of all Cade, the deputy sheriff who had tucked tail and run after Sonny's violent death.

"You should be careful," Wynonna said now, and for a minute Reno thought she meant in regards to Cade. "Those poachers mean business. I didn't say anything earlier because it would've been no use trying to stop you. I understand what the mustangs mean to you, but I also understand what they mean to the poachers. Money. And greed makes men do rash, crazy things."

"I know." Reno nodded. Riding out alone at night wasn't the smartest thing she'd ever done.

And shooting out the ATV headlights? Plain stupid. At the time she'd been too angry to care if she ended up hitting the poachers, who'd had no qualms about shooting at her. Really, really stupid. She could've killed someone. Her passion for the horses had overridden everything else.

Reno sighed. "I'm tired. I'm going to bed."

"Aren't you going to call Austin and tell him what you saw?"

"It's late, and the poachers are gone for now. I'll call him tomorrow."

"Okay," Wynonna said, resigned. "Then I will see you in the morning."

"Good night." Reno turned toward the hall.

"Reno?"

She looked back over her shoulder.

"Don't lose sleep over Cade."

"Not to worry," she replied. "I've got a dream catcher hanging over my bed."

She left hearing Wynonna's soft chuckle, and wondering if the webs of the dream catcher would be strong enough to trap the nightmare of Cade Lantana being back in her life.

CHAPTER TWO

CADE SHOOK OFF the remnants of a nightmare he hadn't had in quite some time. Chalk it up to coming home to Eagle's Nest. Throwing back the covers, he stood, taking in the familiar room.

Home. In Colorado.

It felt strange yet comforting to be on the Diamond L after nine years of living on the outskirts of New Meadows, Idaho. He hadn't expected to feel comforted, plagued as he still was by the events that had led to his departure. He only wished he'd come here under more pleasant circumstances. It killed him to see his father so sick.

After a quick shower, Cade dressed and yanked on his boots—still damp from last night's downpour—and clomped down the stairs. The aroma of coffee and hot, buttered pancakes wafted from the kitchen, drawing him in. His father sat at the table, dressed in his usual Western shirt, jeans and cowboy boots. But the light was gone from his blue eyes. His tan had faded, and he looked as ill as he was. The oxygen tube clipped to his nostrils called attention to his labored breathing.

Cade forced a smile. "Morning, Dad. Mom."

Estelle stood on tiptoe to kiss his cheek. Her short, silver-blond hair smelled like strawberries. "It sure is good to see you in my kitchen, son. Sit down, I've got pancakes ready."

She scowled and pointed a finger at her husband, who'd pulled a cigarette from his shirt pocket and stuck it between his lips. "Light that, Matthew Lantana, and I'll kick your butt—if your oxygen tank doesn't blow you to kingdom come first!"

"Don't get your britches in a knot, woman." Clutching the unfiltered cigarette between two fingers, Matt waved it in the air. "I just wanna suck on the damn thing. Is that all right with you?" He glared at her. "Wasn't gonna light it."

Estelle gave him a dark look. "You're playing with fire either way," she said. "Just tempting and tormenting yourself, is all you're doing." She slammed down a plate with a single pancake in front of him. Refilled his cup. "You shouldn't even have those cancer sticks in the house."

"Can we please not argue on my first morning here?" Cade interjected. "Dad, put the cigarette away."

"Fine." Matthew stuck it back in his shirt pocket. "A man can't do a blasted thing in his own home," he grumbled.

"You can die in your own home, that's what you can do, if you don't stop it!" Estelle blinked, tears rimming her red eyes. She dropped into a chair across from her husband and dug viciously into her own stack of pancakes with the side of her fork.

Purposely and with relish, Matthew put a huge dollop of butter on his single flapjack, then poured enough syrup over it to drown a mule. He narrowed his eyes at Estelle as if daring her to object.

Cade sighed. "Do you feel like taking a ride with me today, Dad?"

"I can't manage horseback anymore—you know that." Without looking at him, Matt shoved a forkful of dripping pancake into his mouth. Though he owned a portable oxygen tank small enough to fit behind a saddle, the limited air supply kept him from riding, since anything less than two hours in the saddle was, in his mind, a waste of time. Not to mention that pride wouldn't allow him to do something with difficulty that had once been second nature.

"I meant a ride in the truck," Cade said. "I'm driving out to Wild Horse Ranch to see what those poachers might've left behind."

Matt snapped to attention. "So, they were there last night?"

Cade nodded. "Bold as you please, trying to run the herd into a canyon."

"That disgusts me to no end," Estelle fumed.

"Can't the sheriff get them for trespassing on Reno's ranch, at least?"

"Yep, but trespassing charges aren't going to solve the problem. The Bureau of Land Management needs to bust them for poaching and theft of government property. But what I hear from Sam Grainger, the agents have been busy out by De Beque, where this same thing's been happening."

"Think it's wise to be poking around on Reno Blackwell's place?" Matt asked. He'd been well aware of Cade's feelings for Reno, and the complicated decision he'd made in leaving Colorado.

Cade shrugged. "Reckon I owe her all the help I can give."

"You're an agent in Idaho, not here," his mother reminded him. "I hate to see you hanging around Reno again." She didn't have to finish what he knew she was thinking. That by leaving, he'd hurt Reno, a teenage girl who'd looked up to him.

But the older Reno had got, the more Cade's interests had changed from brotherly to something more, especially once she turned eighteen. Yet after what her stepfather had done, not to mention what Sonny had forced Cade to do, there was nowhere for those feelings to go. Twenty-five-year-old men weren't supposed to be attracted to eighteen-year-old girls.

"I'm not hanging around with her, Mom. I'm just doing what needs to be done."

"I suppose," Estelle said, "but there's no sense in you dragging your father out in the middle of nowhere."

"For crying out loud!" Matt slammed his cup down, sloshing coffee onto the gingham tablecloth. "Why don't you just go ahead and put me in a pine box and bury me?"

"Matthew, calm down."

"Don't tell me to calm down," he wheezed. Suddenly, a coughing fit seized him, and Cade half rose from his chair, feeling responsible.

"You okay, Dad?" he asked, laying a hand on his arm.

"Oh, Matt." Estelle scooted her own chair away from the table and wrapped an arm around his shoulders. "Relax. Just breathe easy."

"Br—breathe easy," Matt wheezed. "Easy for you…to say." His color had gone from red to ashen, then slowly returned to normal as he leaned back in his chair and sucked in oxygen.

Cade felt like crap. He wished there was something he could do for his father. "I didn't mean to upset you."

"You didn't," Matt snapped. "She did." He waved Estelle away. "Quit fussing, woman. If I'm gonna die, then so be it. But I damn sure ain't gonna sit around this kitchen twenty-four-seven—like an invalid." He breathed somewhat easier. "Yeah, I'll ride along to Wild Horse Ranch with you, son." He reached out to squeeze Cade's hand, and his grip was surprisingly strong. "It's good to have you home, boy."

Cade swallowed the lump in his throat. "It's good to be here, Dad." To his mother he added, "Don't worry. I'll look after him. The truck's air-conditioned, so he'll really be more comfortable in my Chevy than he is in this kitchen." He winked at his father.

The old ranch house was cooled by the shade of the massive cottonwoods that grew around the perimeter of the yard, front and back. Plus most of the rooms had ceiling fans and plenty of windows for cross breezes.

Matt smiled, more like his old self. "I've always been a Ford man myself, but I guess a body can't be choosey."

THE PHONE RANG, startling Reno from her spot in front of her home office computer. She used the PC to keep records of the mustangs that lived at her sanctuary, as well as for her own small herd of fifteen quarter horses.

"Wild Horse Ranch."

"Hey, Reno," Sheriff Pritchard said. "Hope I'm not calling too early."

His sexy drawl gave her shivers. "Not at all. What can I do for you, Austin?"

"Now there's a loaded question," he teased. "I

saw Wynonna at the diner today—talk about a morning person." He laughed and Reno joined him.

"Wy definitely gets up with the chickens." Wynonna sometimes ate breakfast in town on the weekend, lingering over coffee at the diner to chat with her friends.

"Anyway, she told me about your encounter with the poachers."

Reno knew where this was going. Austin wouldn't be at all happy to know Cade was stepping on his toes.

"I would've called you out if I'd been certain they would try something," she said. "I was just following a hunch I had."

"Yeah, well, your hunches can get you into trouble, Reno. You need to let me handle this."

"Actually, there was a BLM ranger out there last night," she said. "I'm sure you remember Cade Lantana." Austin had become a deputy shortly before Cade hung up his badge.

"He's with the BLM now? I thought he'd moved to Idaho."

"He did, so I guess he's not here officially. From what I understand, though, he's got an agent friend in the Glenwood Springs office—Sam Grainger."

"I know Sam," Austin said. "He's a straight-up guy."

"Cade took a leave of absence to come help his mom and dad."

"Yeah, I guess Estelle could use him here," Austin said. "Well, the BLM may have authority over the wild horses, but I'm the law in this county. I'm coming out to have a look around."

"Fine by me." What was it to her if the two men got into a pissing contest? Besides, she enjoyed Austin's company. "Come on up to the house and we can ride out to where the poachers were."

"Will do. See you in a bit, then."

Reno hung up the cordless and had no sooner turned back to the computer when the phone rang again. She picked it up and spoke without preamble. "If you're wanting coffee, I've got the pot on."

"Well, that's mighty thoughtful of you. I can always use a cup."

The deep, familiar voice prickled the hair on the back of her neck. "Cade. I thought you were someone else."

"Does that mean I don't get any coffee?"

She stiffened. How could he banter with her? "That all depends."

"On…?"

"Whether or not Sheriff Pritchard drinks it up."

Silence stretched across the line. "Austin Pritchard? He's sheriff now?"

"Martinez retired shortly after you left. I would've thought your mom told you that."

"We try not to talk much about the past."

Reno ignored her churning stomach.

"So, Pritchard's there—at your place?"

What was that she detected in Cade's voice? Surely not the jealousy she imagined. Must be the macho territorial thing again. "No, but he's on his way over."

"You called him about the poachers?"

"No." She drew the word out into two syllables. "Small town—news spreads fast. Remember?"

"He doesn't need to poke around in this," Cade said. "The BLM—"

"What did you want me to do, Cade? Ground him?"

He merely grunted. "Sam Grainger's up in De Beque today, meeting with a couple of agents from the Grand Junction office." Sam had gone to high school with Cade. "So I thought I'd drive out to your place and take a look around for him. My dad's coming with me. I figured we'd take the back road and come in on the side of your property closest to the river. Maybe drive down near the canyon?"

"Fine by me. Who am I to interfere with what Sam wants you to do?"

"Well, it's your property," he grumbled. "Just thought I'd make a courtesy phone call."

"I'm taking Austin out there on horseback," Reno said. "I figured we'd get a better look around that way."

"Suit yourself. Guess I'll see you out there, then."

"Okay. Bye." She hung up the phone, then glared at it.

Great. Just what she needed. Cade poking around on her ranch. Of course, she'd known that was bound to happen. Even if he didn't have official jurisdiction here, the BLM was a federal agency, and like any other brotherhood of the law. That didn't make having him around any easier. Suddenly Reno was glad Austin was coming out. He could act as a buffer between her and Cade.

At a knock on the kitchen's outside door, she hurried to let Austin in. "Morning, Sheriff. I've got your coffee waiting."

"Appreciate it." He smiled broadly at her, removing his hat. "And if you don't mind my saying so, Reno, you're looking lovely this morning. I'd say red's your color." He indicated the bright crimson, sleeveless Western shirt she wore.

"Thanks," Reno said, pleased. She knew Austin liked her in red.

But then, so had Cade.

Reno shook off the thought. She barely had time for one man in her life, much less two.

And she sure didn't need Cade messing with her head again.

CHAPTER THREE

"ARE YOU SURE you'll be okay here, Dad?" Now that they were at Wild Horse Ranch, his father looked frail, if happy, sitting in the truck, his portable oxygen tank resting on the floorboards.

"Of course I will, son." Matthew relaxed in the luxurious, upholstered seat of the Chevy pickup, leaning back against the headrest. "Don't start sounding like your mother." He smiled.

"I shouldn't be long," Cade said, strapping on his shoulder holster. The semiautomatic .45 pistol inside was loaded with nine rounds, and he had an extra clip in his pocket. "The keys are in the ignition, if you decide to turn on the air." They'd parked in the shade of a canyon, and the morning was cool. "Here's my cell phone if you need it. The reception up here can be sketchy, but—"

"Damn it, go on." Matt waved him away. "I know how to work a cell phone."

"All right." Cade climbed out of the truck.

The sound of flowing water grew louder as he

hiked closer to the Roaring Fork. There was a spot downstream a short way where the river pooled into a watering hole. According to Sam, the mustangs frequented the place, along with deer and elk. Picking his way through the sagebrush and scrub oak, Cade soon found it.

Sure enough, hoofprints lined the water's edge. Fresh manure indicated the mustangs had watered here as recently as this morning, which surprised him, considering the scare the poachers had given the herd the night before. Apparently, the horses' habits were deeply ingrained, and that could prove to be both good and bad. It would allow him to keep watch over them, but give the poachers equal opportunity to come back and find the mustangs easily.

Cade took his digital camera out of his denim jacket. It was a nice one, and he shot both stills and video footage of the watering hole. Then he moved through the brush, winding his way down the canyon toward the spot where he and Reno had run across the poachers. He found an area where ATV tracks crisscrossed through the mud, and saw shattered headlight glass on the ground in a couple of places.

He recalled the shots Reno had exchanged with the poachers. He hadn't thought to berate her last night, but she was going to get herself hurt if she wasn't careful. After taking pictures of the broken glass, Cade gingerly picked it all up and wrapped it inside his bandanna-style handkerchief. It wouldn't do to leave the glass for the mustangs— or any other animal—to step on. He'd show the digital pictures and the glass to Sam.

So intent was he on what he was doing, it took Cade a moment to notice the hoofbeats coming his way. Mustangs? His heart jumped, until he heard the unmistakable sound of a horseshoe striking against rock. A moment later, Reno rode into view on the same blue roan he'd seen last night—when she'd stared at him as though she'd seen a ghost. Cade could hardly blame her. He supposed in some ways that's exactly what he was to her. Had his actions all those years ago haunted her the way they'd haunted him?

Still, he couldn't help but smile at the sight of her. Until he saw Sheriff Pritchard riding behind her on a big sorrel horse. Cade's smile turned into a scowl.

"Morning, Cade," Reno said, not meeting his eyes.

"Look what the cat dragged back to town," Austin said. "It's been a while, Lantana."

"That it has." Cade narrowed his eyes. "There wasn't any need for you to ride all the way out here. Sam's got this investigation under control."

"Well, Sam's not here, and seeing as how I'm the sheriff of this county, I'd say it's my sworn duty to uphold the law under all circumstances, including this one." Austin's pale blue eyes stared back at him.

As cocky as Cade remembered.

"Would you two knock it off," Reno said. "Find anything interesting, Cade?"

"Tire tracks from the ATVs. Looks like there were three or four of them."

"I know I shot out the headlights on two," Reno stated.

Cade started to tell her why that hadn't been a good idea, then decided not to get into it in front of the sheriff.

"I did *not* just hear that," Austin said. "Reno, you can't be out here shooting at people, even if they are trespassing."

"They shot at me first. Besides," Reno said, "I didn't shoot at *people*. I shot their lights. They need to stay off my property. Don't they know about Colorado's Make My Day law? Some property owners would shoot a trespasser pretty quick in these parts."

Austin looked as if he was going to argue the point further, but Cade cut him off. "I was just getting ready to walk upriver a ways."

"What for?" Austin asked, resting one arm against his saddle horn, as the sorrel gelding cocked a hind leg and relaxed beneath him.

"To check out a hunch." Cade started walking

again, eyes carefully scanning the ground. He found the spot where the canyon narrowed, where the poachers had attempted to drive the mustangs into the trap they'd set for them. The shod hoof-prints of his own horse and Reno's were mixed with the ATV tracks. The muddy ground was churned up from all the activity of the night before, clumps of sagebrush trampled.

"Looks to me like they set up a portable fence here to corral the herd," Austin said, from the back of his horse.

No shit, Sherlock.

"What exactly are you looking for?" Reno asked.

Cade hated to share his theory with Austin Pritchard, but then he supposed two heads—three in this case—might be better than one. "Trailer tracks. I have a feeling those ol' boys were plan-ning to haul as many horses out of here last night as they could. Before we came along and inter-rupted their fun."

Reno's eyes widened. "I'd assumed they were going to drive them into the canyon and fence them off, then come back later."

"Could be," Cade said. "But I don't think so. I talked to Sam before I drove out here. The poachers have been hard to catch, and they know the BLM is onto them. I'd bet they'd want to get in and out as quickly as possible."

"Where in the world would somebody park a sizable rig out here?" Austin pondered. "They'd have to leave it up where you parked, and that would make it mighty hard to turn around. That road's not wide."

Cade had already thought of that. "I don't think that's where they left their rigs."

"Where, then?" Reno asked. She'd dismounted and now walked alongside Cade, leading the blue roan.

Her proximity made Cade feel too warm in the light jacket he wore. She smelled like wildflowers, and he noticed that beneath her black cowboy hat, her black braid hung nearly to her waist. She'd always worn her hair long, and the silk of it used to nearly drive him crazy whenever she let her hair fall free. He pushed away the image of an eighteen-year-old Reno.

"According to my topo map," Cade said, "there's a place upriver shaped like a bowl in the rocks, and a road leads from there to the one up above. They could've parked a rig in that bowl and had plenty of room to turn around."

"I know the spot," Reno said. "But the track leading out is pretty hairy. Still, it's worth a look."

"Glad you approve." Cade hadn't intended to say that so sarcastically. He supposed he was annoyed because of Austin breathing down his neck, and Reno stirring up old feelings.

She frowned. "Hey, I'm just here to be an extra pair of eyes," she said.

Cade said nothing, but thought he saw Austin smirk.

Farther along, the ground became less trampled, but the ATV tracks continued on. Cade followed them until he found exactly what he'd been looking for. The small meadow, surrounded by canyon walls, lay at the end of a road resembling a wagon trail more than anything else.

Satisfied, Cade studied the flattened brush and tall grass. A rig had been here, all right, and not just one. From the appearance of the tire tracks, two heavy-duty trucks pulling what were likely roomy, fifth-wheel trailers had parked here last night. Cade took more pictures and video, working his way up to the road, careful not to disturb any evidence.

"I can get my deputies out here to cast and mold those tire tracks," Austin said, when they came to an area where the road was still damp but drying fast. The tracks here were quite clear.

Begrudgingly, Cade nodded. "Be a good idea," he said. "Can you get a copy for Sam?"

Austin lifted a shoulder. "I suppose, though I don't see why that's necessary. I told you, this is my county."

"And this is BLM business," Cade contended.

"Okay, you two boys go ahead and kick sand in each other's faces," Reno said, swinging back onto her gelding. "I'm going to ride farther up this road and see what's what."

With a final dark look Pritchard's way, Cade kept walking, wishing now he had brought his horse.

"Care to swing up behind?" Austin halted the sorrel alongside him, and offered a hand. Cade read the mockery in the man's eyes.

"Thanks, I can walk."

"Suit yourself." Austin rode after Reno, and Cade plodded after them, feeling both irritated and foolish. He'd thought about hauling Jet up here, since his trailer was a two-horse, trickier to back up than a longer trailer, but requiring less space to maneuver. But he'd decided it would be easier to examine the tracks and other possible clues left behind by the poachers if he were on foot, even if it did take a little longer to cover ground. Leave it to Austin to one-up him.

Cade peeled off his jacket and continued his mission. From the looks of things, there had to indeed have been three or four poachers, if the telltale ATV tracks were any indication. By the time he reached the upper road, Cade had no doubt the poachers had used this escape route. He hadn't noticed their tracks as he and his dad drove in, because the poachers had taken the left-hand fork, not toward town, but away. They'd followed back roads out of the area, and would've taken the horses who knew where if he and Reno hadn't stopped them.

Pausing to catch his breath, Cade noted that only one set of shod hoofprints led in that direction now. The other went right toward where he'd left his truck parked. Frowning, he took the right fork, as well, and within a couple of minutes came in sight of it, along with Reno and her horse. She'd dismounted, and was chatting with Matt through the open window of the Chevy.

Pritchard must've continued tracking the poachers. Let him waste his time. He'd end up riding into the next county if he planned to follow those tire tracks.

As Cade drew closer to the truck, the sound of Reno's soft laughter filled the air. Ignoring a stirring of old feelings, he tossed his jacket inside the cab, then leaned over the pickup bed and opened a small cooler he'd placed there. "Want a bottle of water?" he asked Reno. "Dad?"

"No, thanks," Reno said.

"I'm good," Matthew answered. Cade noticed some color in his dad's cheeks. The outing had been good for him. He was obviously enjoying Reno's company.

Cade walked around to the passenger side, admiring the blue roan and wondering if he was a mustang. He studied the gelding's legs and his large, black hooves. Black hooves generally chipped less easily than the light ones on horses with white stockings. The gelding shifted, and Cade frowned, eyeing the rear hoof on the off side.

"Your horse threw a shoe," he said, handing his water to Reno.

"What?" She turned to look for herself. "Crap, I just had those shoes put on a week ago."

"It happens," Matthew said.

"You can't ride him that way," Cade pointed out. A horse could wear two shoes, as long as they were both on the front or on the rear. One odd shoe would put the animal off balance, at risk of going lame.

"I know that," Reno said, not hiding her irritation.

"I'd pull the other hind shoe for you," he offered, "but my farrier tools are in my trailer."

Reno swore under her breath, just as Austin rode up on his sorrel. "Morning, Matt," he called. "You doing all right?"

"I'd be better if I was sitting in the saddle instead of in this fancy truck," Matthew said.

"What's up?" Austin asked Reno.

"Plenty Coups threw a shoe."

The sheriff chewed his bottom lip. "Not good. You want to swing up behind me? We can pony him back to the ranch."

"I'll drive her home," Cade said. "It'll be easier for you to pony the gelding without riding double."

One time, at the fairgrounds when Reno was

seventeen, he'd given her a ride on a frisky buckskin mare he'd recently bought. Reno had snugged up behind him on the back of his saddle, her arms tight around his waist. It was the first time he'd begun to think of her as anything other than the little sister she wanted him to see her as. He'd made the mare prance, so Reno would hang on tighter.

No way did he want Pritchard taking her home.

"DO YOU MIND?" Reno asked Austin, holding Plenty Coups's reins out to the sheriff.

She didn't miss the dark look he gave Cade before Austin smiled at her. "Not at all." He took hold of the split reins. "Guess I'll meet y'all back at the ranch. Good seeing you, Matt."

"Same here." The old rancher nodded, then slid over to the middle of the Chevy's fold-down bench seat to make room.

She climbed in, saddened by the sight of his oxygen tank.

"Hope that blasted thing's not in your way," Matt apologized. "Just scoot it over."

"It's fine," Reno said, arranging her long legs around the tank.

"So, what'd you two find?" Matt asked as Cade started the engine and drove farther down the road, looking for a spot wide enough to turn around.

Cade told him about the trailer tracks. "Also, I

heard around town that an older-model, black-and-silver truck was seen in the area recently, hauling a six-horse trailer. Someone saw it near De Beque, too."

"We've got to stop these guys," Reno declared, her anger rising. "I don't understand how people can stoop so low."

"Makes two of us," Cade said.

"Lots of bad folks out there." Matt shook his head. "I hate to see this happening to the mustangs."

"Nothing's going to happen to them if I can help it," Reno stated.

Back at the ranch house, Reno got out of the truck, then hesitated, leaning on the open door. "You sure you don't want something cold to drink, Matt?" He looked so pitiful, with the oxygen tubes, his worn-out body. But his eyes were sparkling, and Reno had a feeling he hadn't been anywhere in a while. She knew she hadn't seen him in town in ages. "I've got sun tea. Better than bottled water any day." She grinned.

"You've got that right. What fool ever started paying for something you can get right out of your faucet?" He glared at Cade as though the bottled water movement were his fault. "My daddy's probably up there having a laugh at that one." He lifted his chin to nod the brim of his dark brown Stetson skyward.

"I'm sure he is." Reno had heard tales of the

tough rancher who'd raised Matt to be a top-rate hand. "So, what do you say, cowboy? We can sit on the porch and enjoy the morning before it gets any hotter."

"We really ought to get back, Dad," Cade said. "Mom will worry."

But Matt was already halfway out of the truck. "Let her."

"Here, I'll help you with that." Reno reached for the oxygen tank.

"I've got it." Matt waved her away. He wheezed as he stepped down from the Chevy, setting the wheel-mounted tank on the ground and walking with Reno toward the house.

She avoided Cade's eyes, leading the way up the steps, knowing Matthew would take offense if she stood back to let him go first. "Make yourselves at home," she said, indicating the rocker and two ladder-back chairs, one on either side of the front door. "I'll be right with you."

Inside the kitchen, Reno lifted the jar of tea from the refrigerator and poured some into three plastic tumblers she filled with ice. She cut lemon slices and stuck one on the edge of each glass, wondering if Matt took sugar. She didn't, and she remembered that Cade didn't, either. Just in case, she scooped up Wynonna's sugar bowl and set it on a tray.

Balancing her load, Reno went out to the porch.

As she nudged the screen door open with one shoulder, Cade caught it and held it for her. Suddenly she felt shaky. What was with her? He was the same Cade she'd always known.

"Here you go, Matt." Reno set the tray on a small round table between the rocker he'd settled into and one of the chairs. She dropped down next to him, leaving Cade to sit on the other side of the door. Instead, he pulled the chair closer, facing out toward the surrounding mountains.

"That's quite a view," Matt commented.

They made small talk until Austin rode up, leading Plenty Coups. Reno set down her empty glass and went to meet him. "Thanks, Austin," she said, taking the blue roan's reins. "I sure appreciate your help with my horse."

"No problem." He looked toward the porch. "Y'all having a tea party?" he drawled.

Reno grunted. "I guess we are. Want a glass? It's nice and cold."

"Don't mind if I do." Austin swung down from the sorrel, replaced the bridle with a nylon halter and lead rope, and tethered him to the horse trailer parked in the driveway.

"Help yourself," Reno said. "You know where the fridge is."

"Bring me a refill, Austin, will you?" Cade asked, with a thin smile. "Since you seem to be the knight in shining armor today."

The sheriff chuckled, but the sound seemed forced, and Reno turned her back on the pair to lead her horse to the barn. They were acting like a couple of high school boys, trying to impress a girl. But then, she often wondered if the male gender ever grew up.

After caring for Plenty Coups and turning him out into a paddock behind the barn, Reno returned to find the three men in a deep discussion about the poachers.

"I've got everyone on the force keeping their eyes peeled for anything even remotely suspicious," Austin was saying as Reno sat in the chair Cade vacated for her. "And I'll bet the poachers know it. I'd say they aren't likely to strike again for a while. You probably scared them off last night."

"Maybe," Cade said. "But it won't hurt to keep a sharp eye out."

"That's what they'll be expecting," Austin said. "For us to be watching. Of course, it's always good to be cautious." He drained his glass. "Sorry to drink and run, Reno," he said, setting the tumbler on the table. The ice cubes rattled, and as an after-thought, the sheriff fished one out and popped it into his mouth to chew on. "Tell Sam to keep me posted," he mumbled around the ice cube.

"Yeah, sure." But Cade wore a stubborn expression.

Wynonna pulled into the yard in her beat-up

GMC pickup as Austin was loading the sorrel into his trailer. They exchanged greetings before the older woman climbed the porch steps, carrying a couple of shopping bags.

"Need help with that?" Cade asked, rising.

"Heavens no, it's just a few groceries. How are you, Matt?"

"Been better," the cowboy said.

"Well, let's pray you're on the mend," Wynonna declared, the false hope sliding off her tongue as slick as wax on a snowboard.

As she passed Reno, she raised a curious eyebrow that said, *We'll talk about this later.* Reno knew Wy would have fun teasing her about drawing the attention of two good-looking, single cowboys. Having tea on her porch at that.

I was thinking of Matt, Reno would argue.

Uh-huh.

Or maybe a cowboy with blue-green eyes. One she seemed to be harboring a new kind of feeling for, in spite of their muddy past.

CHAPTER FOUR

CADE DROVE HIS FATHER home, unable to get Reno out of his head. Not to mention the way Austin Pritchard had looked at her. The man rubbed him the wrong way. Always had, even though they'd worked together only a short while before Cade quit the sheriff's department. Austin was cocky, and he'd had what women called fast hands. Back in the day, on more than one occasion, Cade had seen him get grabby with the ladies after a couple beers in the bar. And the guy had had an eye for Reno years ago, even though he was only a year younger than Cade himself.

Jackass.

"I enjoyed that," Matt said. "Thanks, son."

Cade focused on the road. He knew how hard it was for his dad to admit his limitations. Putting up with Austin was well worth the effort if the outing gave Matt even a few moments' pleasure. "Glad to have your company, Dad."

Matthew harrumphed. "If your mother had her

way, I'd be in some damn hospital lying flat on my back, waiting to die."

"Don't you think you're being hard on her?" Cade asked. He hated the rift that seemed to grow between his parents with each passing day. Estelle couldn't hide her anger that the man she loved and had been married to for nearly forty years had smoked his way closer to his grave. "Be patient, Dad. Mom only wants what's best for you."

"In her own way, I suppose she does. But it's not my way."

Stubborn old cowboy. Yet, like it or not, Cade could relate.

"Sam's thinking about camping out near the watering hole," he said, changing the subject. "Keep a closer eye on the mustangs that way. I might go with him, if you and Mom can spare me for a little while."

"Those horses are gonna find someplace else to water if you spook them," Matt said, "not to mention the poachers aren't likely to return to the same spot, when they know you saw them there."

"It's a place to start. I'll take Jet up there with me, and one of your packhorses, if that's okay. Sam will be on horseback. Maybe the herd will be curious enough about the geldings to stick around for a bit. If not, then I guess Sam will ride after them wherever they go. I'd sure like to help him," he repeated. Actually, helping catch the poachers had a great deal to do with Reno. Cade owed her. If he could in some small way make up for the past, maybe he'd sleep better at night, and God knew she loved those mustangs.

He couldn't be gone on a long stakeout, since he'd come here to help his parents with the Diamond L. If only he could clone himself…

"Do what you want," Matt said. "Your mom and I don't expect you to spend every waking minute with us. But she's got a Fourth of July barbecue planned for tomorrow. It's something she's been doing the past several years. She's got all the neighbors coming, and she'll be disappointed if you're not there."

Cade's hands went cold. A barbecue? His mother had never mentioned it to him. *Shit.* That meant he'd have to face all their neighbors in one fell swoop. Neighbors who knew he'd killed Sonny. Some had thought him a hero, others not so much, not after the way he'd left Reno. Either way, he wasn't ready for this. He didn't want to be the center of attention.

It's just a barbecue. Get a grip.

"What time?"

"Five-thirty, thereabouts. After the rodeo."

"All right. But I think I'll still camp out tonight." Riding always put him in a better frame of mind. Maybe he'd feel calmer, more up to facing people afterward. "I'll let Mom know I'll be back in plenty of time to help set things up."

"Guess that'll work."

"Is Reno invited?" The question slipped off his tongue before Cade could stop it.

"I reckon. She's a neighbor, ain't she?" In Eagle's Nest, anyone living in the county was considered a neighbor. "Sure wish I could camp out with you," Matt said, his breathing labored. He looked ready for a nap.

"So do I," Cade said.

As a kid, how many miles had he covered with his dad over the years, riding herd, fixing fence? Enough to stretch coast to coast and then some, he'd wager. He grinned, trying to lighten the mood. "Coming back early will work out all right, anyway. I can't leave you alone too long with Mom distracted. You're bound to sneak a smoke, or maybe try to move the cows by yourself." Cade and Heath—the one ranch hand they had left—were planning to drive the cows and calves to new pasture in the next few days.

"Humph. I wish," his dad grumbled. "Your mother would have my hide tanned into saddle leather, just so she could ride my back even after I'm gone."

Cade couldn't help but laugh. "She loves you."

"I know." Matt reached into his shirt pocket and fished out the single cigarette he kept there. He put it in his mouth and rolled it from side to side. "Man, I miss these confounded things."

Cade grunted. "Why do you torment yourself that way?"

"Sometimes a little torment is worth it," Matt said. "Kind of like you and Reno." To Cade's surprise, a twinkle lit his father's eyes.

"What's that supposed to mean?"

He snorted. "Any fool can see you still care about her."

"It's not like you think," Cade said. "She never thought about me that way, anyhow."

"That was then, this is now."

"Whatever," Cade said. "I owe her, and that's that."

"You didn't make Carlina swallow those pills," Matt said. "Sonny Sanchez did that, as sure as if he'd shoved 'em down her throat." He lowered his voice. "When are you going to stop tormenting *yourself,* son?" He slipped the cigarette back into his shirt pocket and took out a snuff can. "Tell your mother, and I'll tan your hide."

Cade bit his lip.

Not about the chewing tobacco, but against the guilt he still couldn't shake.

If he hadn't shot Sonny, Carlina Sanchez never would have overdosed.

And Reno would've had the mother she'd needed.

RENO CLEANED UP the kitchen, washing the plastic tumblers and sun tea jar. While the clean container filled again beneath the running tap, she reached in the cupboard for tea bags, and noticed the note Wynonna had scribbled on the dry erase board fastened to the fridge: "BBQ—Diamond L—5:30 Sun."

She'd nearly forgotten.

The Lantanas had been putting on an annual Fourth of July barbecue ever since the summer Cade left. Reno wondered if the tradition had started out of guilt or remorse. After all, he hadn't gone under pleasant circumstances. And while a lot of townspeople thought of him as a hero, there were those who weren't so sure.

No matter her own personal feelings, Reno had sympathized with Cade's parents, Estelle in particular. How hard it must seem to be the mother—a mother in a small town—of a man who'd had to shoot and kill someone. Even if your son was a deputy sheriff. Even if the man he shot was a pedophile and a killer.

And even if Sonny Sanchez was the only father Reno had ever known.

Reno raised one eyebrow. The note hadn't been on the fridge earlier.

"Ah, you noticed," Wynonna said from behind her. "I, uh, forgot to remind you before."

"No problem." She turned off the faucet, straightened her shoulders, lifted her chin and knew she wasn't fooling Wy any more than she was fooling herself. "I've gone to Estelle's barbecue for the past nine years. Why shouldn't I go this year?"

"Exactly." Wynonna nodded, relief spreading over her features.

Reno's shoulders slumped. "Who am I kidding, Wy? I *can't* go this year."

Wynonna busied herself drying the tumblers Reno had stacked in the dish drainer. "And why not?"

"You know why."

"It'll be fun. You're going to stand there and tell me you'd let a man—even Cade Lantana—stop you from going?"

Reno pulled the tea bags from their individual wrappers and placed them in the jar. "I think you know the answer to that."

"You have to go. It would be rude if you don't attend."

She didn't want to socialize with Cade. The mustangs were one thing, but…

But she was still pissed at him—her big brother—for leaving her.

"Estelle went to a lot of hard work," Wynonna said. "I've been helping her here and there."

Since Wynonna often went on a baking spree, Reno hadn't really thought much of it when she'd noticed the extra homemade desserts stored in the refrigerator. She was about to protest when the phone rang, making her jump.

"Hello?"

"Hi yourself, gorgeous."

"Austin. What are you up to?"

"About six-one." He laughed.

Reno couldn't help but chuckle. "Ha. You ought to get your own stage act."

"Maybe I will. You want to be my assistant?"

"Nope. I have an aversion to being sawed in half."

"That's a magician's assistant, not a comedian's."

"Comedians don't have assistants."

"Darn. Do they have dates?"

"I don't know. Maybe they prefer raisins."

He laughed again. "Oh, that's bad. But not bad enough to keep me from asking you out."

"Is that right?" Reno wrapped the kitchen phone cord around her index finger. "Where to? If it's Red Lobster, I'm there." There was one in Grand Junction—worth the eighty-five-mile drive.

"Sorry to disappoint you. I was thinking more along the lines of a barbecue—the one at the Diamond L, to be exact."

The Lantanas' barbecue…shit.

Reno cupped the phone with one hand, turning her back on Wynonna, who pretended to be busy putting the dishes in the cupboard.

"You're going?"

"Of course. I always do."

"Well, yeah, but I thought…"

"That Cade would keep me away? Not hardly. He may think he's a big bad BLM agent, but this isn't Idaho."

Reno rolled her eyes. "Austin, you don't have to play macho to me. I'm not impressed and you know it."

"I'm wounded." She could picture him clutching his chest, and she had to smile. "Don't tell me Cade's scared *you* off going?"

"What makes you say that?"

"Oh, I don't know. I think someone had a crush on someone else a long time ago. And I also think I know a pretty woman who got her heart stomped on when that coward left."

"Don't call him that."

"Hey, take it easy. I'm just quoting your grandpa Mel."

Reno's chest burned. "Leave my grandfather out of this," she snapped.

"He should be a man. Stand up for what he did. He wasn't wrong."

Maybe not in shooting Sonny. But Cade had been wrong to leave her. That had broken her heart and angered Grandpa Mel. Reno often wondered if the shooting and her mother's suicide had contributed to her grandfather's decline in health, and ultimately the back-to-back strokes that had killed him.

"And, no," Reno said, "I don't plan on letting Cade Lantana get to me."

"Does that mean you'll go to the barbecue with me then?"

Why not? She enjoyed Austin's company, had even slept with him recently and had found him sexually stimulating, though she wasn't sure she was ready to do it again. They'd both agreed to back off and take things more slowly, though at times Austin was bad about keeping his hands to himself.

And she sure wasn't about to let Cade dictate where she could and couldn't go. Her earlier reservations slipped away as a feeling of spite and power replaced them.

"Yes," she said. "I'll go with you. It'll be fun."

"Good." She could hear the smile in Austin's voice. "I look forward to it. And don't forget, the first dance is mine."

"Depends on whether or not Matthew McConaughey shows up this year."

Austin guffawed. "Pick you up at five?"

"See you then." Reno hung up the phone and faced Wynonna, who stood with hands clasped like an eager child.

"So you're going?"

"Yes, I am."

"Excellent. Go look in your room. I made something for you for the barbecue, and I don't mean fudge brownies."

Reno stood with elbows akimbo. "Wynonna Left Hand Bull."

"You'll like it." The older woman's cheeks dimpled. "And so will Austin. Or maybe Cade."

Reno frowned, but set the sun tea jar out on the porch, then went upstairs to her room. On the bed was a gift box tied with ribbon. She lifted the lid, pushed the tissue paper aside and gasped.

Wynonna was right. She loved it. Of stone-washed denim, the skirt was hand stitched with intricate beadwork and embroidery along one side—of horses and Native American symbols. And on the opposite side, over the slit pocket, was Reno's Indian name Grandpa Mel had lovingly christened her with: Swift Horse.

Standing in front of the full-length mirror on her closet door, Reno held the skirt against her waist. It hung to midcalf, and would look stunning with her black, Western dress boots.

"Do you like it?" Wynonna asked from the doorway.

"I love it." Reno gave the older woman a hug. "Thank you so much. But you shouldn't fuss over me this way."

"It's my job to fuss," Wy said. "Besides, you'll look wonderful in it, especially if you wear it with your lavender blouse."

What would Reno have done without Wynonna all these years? Bless her big, kind heart.

Busy with the ranch, Reno had rare occasion to get gussied up. She wasn't one for anything too fancy, but it was fun to put on a nice skirt and a little makeup once in a while. She smiled into the mirror. Wynonna was obviously still trying to play matchmaker, one way or another. But at any rate, the skirt meant so much, lovingly sewn by Wy's own hands. The woman could sew even better than she could cook, and that was saying a lot.

Reno definitely planned to skip tomorrow's rodeo. Instead, she'd spend the day riding, keeping watch over the herd once her morning chores were done. But it might be fun to get out for the evening. Even if it meant being around Cade.

In fact, it would be fun to watch him squirm when she walked through the door with Austin.

"Perfect. And I've got just the right earrings, too."

Eat your heart out, Cade Lantana.

"MAYBE WE OUGHT TO ROLL up the windows to keep from messing your hair." Austin sat behind the wheel of his Dodge Ram, looking sexy in a black Western shirt, gray cowboy hat and boots.

Reno had left her long hair loose. She loved the way the wind felt, blowing across her face. Almost like flying along on Plenty Coups. She would never understand why people rode in a closed-up, air-conditioned vehicle.

"It'll comb out," she said. "It's too hot to shut the windows, and you know I hate air-conditioning."

He laughed. "You're an original, Reno, that's for sure." He eyed her before focusing on the road again. "You ought to dress up more often."

"You're pretty hot yourself, cowboy."

At the Diamond L, the driveway was already filling. Reno felt a wave of nostalgia as Austin found a parking spot, and Wynonna—who'd insisted on driving herself—pulled in behind them. So little had changed over the years, it was like stepping back in time.

As she and Austin strode up the walkway with Wynonna, carrying Wy's covered desserts, Reno recalled the time she'd ridden her palomino mare to the Diamond L, where Cade was in the arena honing his bronc-busting on a practice horse—a rangy Appaloosa that bucked like nobody's business.

"Hey, kid," he'd said, dusting off the seat of his pants after his intended eight-second ride ended prematurely. "What'd you do, ride that pony all the way over here just to watch me?"

"I ride my horse everywhere. Five miles is nothing."

Back then, at fifteen years old, she'd often ridden from sunup to sundown. Still, Reno would've ridden five hundred miles to get the attention of the cowboy she looked up to….

"Hi," Cade said as he opened the front door now. He frowned when he saw Austin beside her.

For a moment, a reply stuck in Reno's throat. She'd half expected to look up and see Cade on a bronc. Not to mention she'd figured Estelle would answer the door.

Damn. His boots made him seem even taller than six foot two. He wore a black cowboy hat, not the beat-up, everyday Resistol he'd had on yesterday, but one that looked as if it carried more than a few Xs inside the brim. The more Xs, the better the quality of a cowboy hat, and the higher the price. Cade had always had a thing for an expensive hat and boots.

He wore a maroon Western shirt, with metallic thread and pearl snaps, and his new jeans fit as if someone had poured him into them, like melted chocolate into a mold.

This was the man who'd abandoned her.

And she was with Austin.

With a brief greeting, she brushed past Cade as he held the door, then trailed behind Wynonna as Estelle called to them from the kitchen.

The spacious room had been painted a pale eggshell since last year. The ice-blue, granite countertops were covered with containers of food and stacks of heavy-duty paper plates and disposable flatware.

"Just set those anywhere," Estelle said after

greeting them, nodding toward Wynonna's pans of fudge brownies and pecan pie. "We're going to do a buffet-style food line, then eat outside. The guys have got picnic tables set up."

"What can we do to help?" Reno asked.

"Not a thing," Estelle said. "Go on outside and relax. Help yourselves to a cold drink."

"This way, ladies." Ignoring Austin, Cade gestured toward the sliding doors to the patio. When Reno passed through the screen door, she got a good whiff of the cologne he wore.

Instead of turning her on, it only irritated her. How dare he come home and act as if nothing had happened? Austin smacked her playfully on the butt as they stepped onto the deck, and she took his hand, diverting him, as they walked outside.

"There's beer, pop and bottled water," Cade said, frowning as his gaze fell on their clasped hands. He indicated two large stock tanks filled with ice, between the patio and the rows of picnic tables arranged in the yard beneath a huge canvas tent.

"Now you're talking," Austin said. "Can I get you a beer, Reno?"

"Sounds perfect," she said. She'd intended to have a pop. She caught herself just in time to keep from wiping her sweaty hands on the denim skirt. *Not wearing blue jeans.* But damn, her stomach felt queasy with resentment she'd thought long buried. She shouldn't have come here.

Reno sat with Wynonna at one of the many picnic tables beneath the tent awning, saving a place for Austin.

"Hey, Reno. Wynonna." Ceara Walsh, who ran sheep on the one hundred and fifty acres bordering the Diamond L, looked up as she scooted over to make room for them. "It's been a while. Nice to see you."

"You, too," Wy said.

"Hi, Ceara." Reno admired the older woman for running a ranch alone after losing two husbands, one to a farming accident, the other to cancer.

"Love the skirt. That's your handiwork, isn't it, Wy?"

Wy beamed. "Yes, it is."

Reno slid easily into the conversation, warmed by the feeling of being among friends and neighbors. Sometimes she got so caught up in her work at the ranch, she forgot to socialize.

She tapped her foot to the country music that poured through speakers on a raised deck adjoining the patio. Red, white and blue crepe paper and balloons hung suspended from the tent structure. The shade was a welcome relief from the late-afternoon sun.

Moments later, Austin approached and handed Reno a can of Coors. A chunk of ice clung to the outside, and Reno's mouth watered. She didn't drink very often, but there was nothing quite like a cold beer on a hot summer day, especially at a barbecue.

"Matthew looks well today," she said, popping the top on her can.

Matt sat on the end of one picnic bench, wearing his Western best, chatting with a group of ranchers Reno knew he'd grown up with. Apparently he was telling them a pretty good story, complete with elaborate gestures and facial expressions that had the cowboys bent double with laughter.

"Yeah, he does," Austin agreed.

Reno took a swig of beer, and a breeze kicked up, blowing a strand of hair across her face. It stuck to her lip gloss, which reminded her that she must look a mess. *Great.*

She stood, tugging at the strand. "Be right back, Austin." Wynonna had wandered off to chat with a group of ladies from her crafts class.

"Beer going through you already?"

Reno turned sharply at the sound of Cade's voice.

His teasing brought to mind the friend he'd once been to her, who'd ribbed her every chance he got. But there was nothing brotherly about him today, not if the tightness in her chest was any indication. A tightness that had more to do with painful memories than attraction.

"I better brush my hair before I scare away your guests. We rode here with the windows down. Excuse me." She slipped past him.

Back outside a few minutes later, she spotted him with a group of cowboys. There was certainly no shortage of attractive men. The Lantanas' ranch hand, Heath, gave her an appreciative glance and a wink as she passed by. Reno smiled back. Cute, but younger than she preferred. Probably barely past twenty-one. She'd seen Heath Wiley around town, chatted with him at the feed store. He was nice enough.

Austin stood and crooked his elbow as she returned to their table. "How about that first dance, pretty lady?"

Near the tent, the spacious wooden deck served as a makeshift dance floor. Reno opened her mouth to say yes.

"Sorry, Pritchard," Cade said from behind her, giving Reno a start. "This one's mine."

He slipped his arm around her waist and guided her up the steps to the deck before she could protest.

This one's mine.

The cowgirl or the dance?

CHAPTER FIVE

"YOU DIDN'T STRIKE ME as the dancing type," Cade said, grasping the first thought he could to take his mind off how good Reno felt—and the fact that she smelled like daisies. She was also wearing makeup. Subtle, but enough to show off her long eyelashes, and bring out the bronze of her skin. He'd never even seen her in anything but blue jeans.

"Then why the hell did you ask me?" Her deep brown eyes pierced him. "To spite Austin?"

He bristled. "Maybe."

She stiffened in his arms. "I don't like being used."

"I didn't mean..." He swallowed a curse. "The guy's a jerk, Reno. What do you see in him?"

"Obviously something I don't see in you." She pulled away from his grasp. "Excuse me. I left a cold beer and a hot cowboy back at my table."

"Reno..."

She left him standing there, fuming, feeling like a complete idiot. He rubbed his neck, which still hurt from sleeping on the cold ground the night before. On top of everything else, he was getting too old for stakeouts.

"Oh, good, I can cut in." At the vaguely familiar voice, he turned to see Maura McPherson at his elbow.

"Hey." He smiled at the cute little blonde who worked at the feed store. "It'd be my pleasure."

A slow George Strait number about a rodeo cowboy in Amarillo began to play, and Cade swept Maura into an easy two-step.

Stealing a glance over her shoulder, he saw Austin slip his arm around Reno's waist and hand her her beer. The guy leaned over and whispered something to her, and Reno laughed. Cade wanted to punch him.

EVEN WYNONNA was cuddled in the arms of a cowboy, Reno thought as she sat beside Austin within view of the dance floor. Reno recognized the older man as a neighboring ranch hand. He had Wy giggling and blushing like a young girl at a 4-H dance.

You go, Wy.

And, of course, there was Cade. Dancing with twenty-five-year-old Maura McPherson. When had he met her? *Let Maura have him.*

Moments later, when the song ended, Maura spotted Reno and headed her way, with Cade on her heels. "Hey, Reno. Hi, Austin. How's it going?" She slid onto the picnic bench across the table.

"Hanging in there," Reno said, reaching for a pretzel from the plastic bowl Austin had placed between them.

"I read the article *Horse & Rider* magazine did on your mustang sanctuary," Maura stated. "Very interesting place you've got, and the photos were great."

It was the second article published about Wild Horse Ranch. *Western Horseman* had done one on Reno and her grandfather in connection with the horses years ago.

"Thanks," she said. "Maybe they'll do one on the poachers."

"There's a thought," Maura exclaimed. "Hey, are you looking for more volunteers at your sanctuary?"

"Always. We usually have at least thirty heads at any given time." Some of the horses were too old, lame or wild for anyone to want to adopt, and had permanent homes at Reno's ranch.

Maura nodded, ponytail bobbing. "That's a handful. I've been meaning to give you a call."

"Your expertise would be welcome," Reno said, taking a swig of beer. She refused to so much as look at Cade, who'd settled beside Maura.

"What expertise is that?" he asked.

"Maura graduated from Front Range Community College with a degree in equine management and training," Austin interjected. "This past spring," he added pointedly.

Cade clearly got the message, and just as clearly didn't appreciate it. A lot of men dated younger women, but Reno knew he wasn't one of them. Sonny Sanchez's sick penchant for underage girls and children had made Cade so ill, he'd run as far and as fast as he could from any woman less than a couple years his junior.

Especially her, with seven years between them.

"Maura's a friend of Mom and Dad's," Cade said, leaning over the table toward Austin. "You got a problem with that?"

"Hey, I'm just explaining her *expertise.*"

"Whoa, boys," Maura said, before Reno could grab them and knock their stupid heads together.

The blonde turned back to her. "You know how much I admire what you're doing, Reno. I'd be honored to help out."

"And I'd be grateful. Come by the ranch anytime." Reno hiccuped. "'Scuse me."

Cade laughed. "Maybe we'd better cut you off, cowgirl. How many have you had?" He eyeballed the Coors can in her hand.

"Two—no, wait, one and a half," Reno said.

"Maybe you'd better switch to Pepsi."

Unable to believe his gall, she narrowed her eyes. "You're not my keeper," she said. "I think we established that a long time ago."

Cade held up his hands in surrender, and Maura glanced from one to the other.

"Ignore him," Reno said. "Wynonna doesn't drink. She can drive me home. Come say hi to her. We can talk more about the horses."

Maura stood, obviously eager to help relieve the tension in the air.

Reno hooked one arm over the girl's neck in a gesture of camaraderie, but over her shoulder she mouthed to Cade, *"Nice try."*

He seemed very confused by that, and even Reno wasn't certain what she meant. Nice try at controlling her drinking, or flirting with Maura?

Didn't matter. No man told her what to do—not since Grandpa Mel had died. And he'd done so out of love and respect. Since she only drank on rare occasions, and this barbecue was one of them, she'd do as she pleased.

Concerning Maura, well, Reno supposed that was none of her business. Let Cade flirt, for all she cared. Besides, Reno liked Maura. She was only two years younger than Reno herself, and Maura's dad, Chet, was a brand inspector, her mother a 4-H leader. Still, walking beside Maura, talking about horses and barrel racing, reminded Reno of her rodeo days, and suddenly she felt old. The weight of her past hung on her shoulders.

She shrugged it off. Nothing was going to spoil this afternoon. She'd come here to be polite, but now she was really having fun as she and Maura sat beside Wynonna.

Austin rejoined them a bit later, massaging the back of Reno's neck with strong fingers. "Did I tell you how hot you look?" he whispered in her ear.

Reno swallowed. She liked Austin—a lot—but they'd agreed to slow things down.

"Soup's on!" Estelle called, literally saving her by ringing an old-fashioned triangle.

"Good Lord, I hope not," Reno said, happy to avoid answering Austin. "I came here for some barbecue!"

Nearby, several cowboys whooped. "Yeah! Where's your prize-winning ribs, Estelle?"

"Estelle, hell!" Matthew kidded, having drunk a few beers of his own. "I may be toting an oxygen tank, and I might not be able to get too close to the grill unless I unhook it…" more whoops sounded "…but I can still fire up the best ribs in Garfield County, and then some. Come and get it, you hungry cowpokes! Ladies first," he wheezed, before succumbing to a coughing spell.

Matt waved everybody away. "I'm fine! If only my dear wife here would let me puff on one lousy cigarette, I'd be right as rain."

Several older cowboys guffawed as Estelle shook a barbecue fork at her husband, and proceeded to give him a butt-chewing.

Buzzed or not, Reno noted the affection in

Estelle's voice—so obvious, she might as well have given Matt a big kiss instead of a prod with the oversize fork.

Cade laughed and walked up behind his mother, squeezing her shoulders. "Don't stick him, Mom," he said. "You'll bend the fork on his tough old hide."

More laughter broke out.

But Reno noticed something else. Several people were staring at Cade with something less than friendliness. Open curiosity to downright hostility, she guessed. And some people looked her way, too.

Did her friends and neighbors so readily sense her resentment toward Cade? Did they really share her view? She didn't blame him for gunning down her stepfather in the shootout nine years ago, when Sonny had holed up in a shack in the woods.

She blamed Cade for leaving her. For not giving a damn about her feelings, or even those of his mom and dad. Poor Matthew and Estelle had been holding their annual barbecue all these summers, like an apology for what their son had done. He'd been a hero for killing a murdering pedophile.

But a coward for turning tail and fleeing.

Reno shook off her melancholy as she picked choice morsels off the buffet table, making sure to get a couple of Matt's famous ribs. He had a secret marinade recipe he refused to divulge. If anyone asked, they always got the same old answer: "I could tell you what's in my secret sauce, but then I'd have to kill you."

Reno even managed to squeeze in a piece of Wynonna's glorious pecan pie, though the final bite left her skirt feeling tight at the waist.

Before she could do more than dispose of her paper plate and plastic utensils, the country music went silent. Heads turned as Austin stepped up to the deck railing, overlooking the picnic tables.

"Can I have everyone's attention for a moment, please?" he called out. The noise of the crowd faded to a murmur as all eyes turned to the sheriff.

"I just got a call from one of my deputies. It seems the poachers have struck again, and this time they managed to get away with a load of horses. Jesse Waylon spotted them at the Quick Stop. They had Storm-Bringer in a six-horse gooseneck." This last he said to Reno.

She gasped. Reno knew the mare well, as did most of the locals, including Jesse, who worked at the Quick Stop. At least twenty years old, the black mustang had been with the herd on Reno's rangeland for as long as she could remember. It sickened her to think the mare her grandfather had named for the unusual lightning bolt blaze on her face had been taken by the poachers. She knew what the old mare's fate was likely to be.

Austin searched the crowd until he found Cade.

"Jesse pumped their gas, and he heard one of them say something about going back to Red Hawk Pointe for a second load. Guess now's not the time to quibble over territory, Lantana. Call Sam Grainger. Why don't y'all meet me and my boys at Red Hawk, pronto. Reno, you can ride along if you want, since it borders your property."

Reno's heart flew into her throat. She knew the mountain like her own backyard. "You'd better know I will."

Cade encouraged his parents' guests to remain at the ranch and enjoy the party, though the sheriff's news had put a damper on everyone's spirits.

"You don't have to go, you know," Cade said to Reno, as she prepared to leave with Austin.

"Grandpa Mel wouldn't have stood by and let poachers take the mustangs, especially Storm. I'm going."

Cade tugged down the brim of his hat. "Guess I figured that."

She'd ride with Austin on this one, all right.

And when she found the men who'd taken her beloved mustangs, Lord help them.

She just might end up in jail herself.

CHAPTER SIX

As CADE CLIMBED BEHIND the wheel of his pickup, he noticed an empty spot near the foot of the driveway where a sharp-looking, older-model Ford truck had been parked earlier. The black-and-silver '79 had caught his eye, and he'd meant to ask his mom who it belonged to, but then Reno had rung the doorbell and his brain had turned to mush.

He didn't know a lot of the vehicles his parents' friends drove anymore. Still, the mention of the truck and trailer noticed in town days before the Fourth of July stuck in his mind. One person who'd seen it had described it as silver with a black trailer; another had said the truck was black and silver. Close enough either way, especially since he knew eyewitnesses often got vehicle descriptions wrong. Then again, why would a poacher come to his mother's barbecue?

It looked as if most of the people had taken his advice to stay and enjoy the party. He hated to see Reno leave, because he could tell she'd literally let down her hair, and he wondered how often, if ever, she let herself do that.

Behind him in the horse trailer, Cade towed Jet. He'd already spoken on his cell phone to Sam, who'd asked him to go ahead to Red Hawk Pointe. Sam and another ranger, Paul Whitaker, would meet him there. The mountain was about three miles as the crow flies from the canyon and watering hole where the poachers had been on Friday. An area Cade and Sam had ridden earlier this morning. Had the poachers been watching them, waiting them out?

By the time Cade found a place to leave his truck and trailer near the mountain named for the local red-tailed hawks, and had saddled Jet, Pritchard's truck and trailer came rattling down the road. For once, Cade didn't mind seeing the guy.

With Sam over an hour's drive away in De Beque, and given how shorthanded they were, he was sure the BLM could use all the help it could get.

RENO STOPPED SHORT of the paddock where Plenty Coups should be, but wasn't. The gate to the enclosure stood open, and her beloved blue roan and the three mustang mares he'd been with, including his dam, Honey, were nowhere to be seen.

Letting out a curse, Reno rushed all the way to the paddock, realizing how agitated her dogs were.

Tank and Willow ran up to her, panting as though they'd been running hard, and Snap and Blue Dog appeared from the sagebrush surrounding the barn, tongues lolling.

"Hey, guys, what's the matter, huh?" Reno murmured as she walked carefully around the paddock's perimeter, examining the ground. Shod hoofprints led away from the gate, disappearing in the grass, and nearby she saw boot tracks.

Someone had either taken her horses or let them out. And from the way her dogs were acting, Reno would bet on the former. Why? Were the poachers so desperate they were now stealing ranch stock, as well? But then, Plenty Coups and the mares were mustangs, tame or not. The eye-catching gelding might've held enough appeal to tempt the poachers. Had they let the mares loose, then taken the blue roan, or stolen them all? Either way, the thieves appeared to have been on horseback. She couldn't imagine them being bold enough to pull a truck and trailer into her driveway to load her stock. Maybe they had known no one was home.

What they might not have bargained on was the dogs. Her little ginger-red mutt, Snap, was normally friendly, but Tank and Willow were excellent watchdogs and would've gone after any trespassers. Same with Blue Dog. The Catahoula mix was forty-five pounds of mean if she sensed a threat, and forty-five pounds of love to anyone she perceived as a friend. Her agitation told Reno she wasn't happy right now. Had she chased them through the brush? Reno bent to pat the dog, burying her nose in the blue merle's short coat. She smelled of the sharp, tangy aroma of sagebrush, and bits of seeds from the plant were stuck to her coat.

Reno brushed them off and, heart pounding, hurried back to the driveway to look for tire marks. But as far as she could tell, the only tracks she spotted in the dirt and gravel belonged to her own truck, or Wynonna's. Not wanting to waste time, with Austin and the others expecting her, Reno went to the paddocks where she kept her rescue mustangs.

She chose a stout gray with a nearly snow-white coat. The dappled mare had come from an adoptive home where she'd been spoiled by owners who taught her bad habits, then returned her to the BLM as "unrideable." It had taken Reno a lot of work to break those habits, and the gray, named Cloud, still bucked now and then. Yet she was tough and sure-footed, and her stamina was amazing.

Reno saddled the mare as quickly as she could, and rode toward Red Hawk Pointe. Cloud crowhopped a little as they made their way through the brush, and Reno lined her out with a sharp nudge of her heels and a tug on the reins. As she rode, the semi-level ground began a gradual incline, and the dense clumps of sagebrush and knee-high grass gave way to rockier soil and more trees.

Piñon juniper dotted the landscape, in some places too thick to ride through. Reno found an opening in the trees and sent Cloud up the hillside. As the stout mare climbed, piñons gave way to pine and the occasional blue spruce. Groves of white-barked aspen stood with leaves whispering in the breeze, creating the unique sound that gave them the nickname "quakies." In the distance above, she could see Red Hawk Pointe, reaching toward the skyline.

She caught up with Cade and Austin a short time later, where they'd halted their horses in a clearing. Cade eyed Cloud. "Where's your roan?"

"Good question." Reno told them what had happened.

Cade let out an expletive. "Plenty Coups is a mustang?"

Reno nodded. She'd owned the horse and his dam since Plenty Coups was a foal. "I adopted all four of those horses from the BLM."

"So now the poachers are going after adopted mustangs, too?" Cade turned to Austin. "They're stooping pretty low."

"Can't get much lower," Austin said, face pinched.

"I can send one of my deputies out to look around." Austin slowed his horse, talking into the radio mike attached to his shirt.

Reno heard hoofbeats behind them, and turned in the saddle to see a cowboy with a salt-and-pepper handlebar mustache approaching on a big bay gelding. *Sam Grainger.* A man with carrot-colored hair rode beside him.

"Hey, Sam. Paul," Cade said in greeting. He introduced Reno to Paul, a new agent. Sam she'd known for years. "Reno's missing some horses."

"That right?" Sam spat a stream of tobacco into the brush as Reno explained.

"I've got deputies covering I-70 in both directions," Austin said, "as well as Highway 6 and 24. The poachers are bound to make a mistake sooner or later."

"They already have," Reno said, setting her jaw, "if they took Plenty Coups."

BY THE TIME she got home, Reno was tired and dirty, and so mad she couldn't see straight. It was almost dark, and Wynonna's truck was parked in the driveway, the ranch house lights on. Once Reno had unsaddled Cloud and brushed the mare down, she went up to the house.

"Austin's deputy was here a while ago," Wy said as soon as she came in. "Did you find Plenty Coups and the mares?"

"No." Reno heaved a weary breath and sank into one of the overstuffed chairs parallel to the couch where Wynonna sat crocheting. Wy always tended to do something with her hands whenever she was nervous or upset. The brightly patterned, violet and dark blue yarn of what looked to be the start of an afghan spread across the woman's lap, trailing onto the hunter-green carpet at her feet. The room felt cool and cozy…inviting. A place where Reno often read, where she'd grown up watching Wynonna create beautiful things like the afghans that had always covered Reno's bed. A place where she'd sat mesmerized for hours while Grandpa Mel told her stories of days past. Reno had called the ranch house—which had been in her family for four generations—home her entire life. It was a place where she'd always felt safe.

Now she felt violated by the thieves who'd stolen her horses.

Wynonna looked as sick as Reno felt. "You think the poachers took them, then?"

"As far as we can figure. I'm going to make some phone calls. Put everybody I can think of between here and the Utah border on alert. Then I need a shower."

"I'll get on the Internet," Wynonna said, all business. "There are e-mail loops for stolen horses. Barry Biltmore was telling me about them tonight at the barbecue."

Reno managed a small smile. "I saw you dancing with him. He's a pretty good-lookin' fella."

Wy blushed. "Go on, now." She waved her hand. "You've got better things to think about than handsome men."

No doubt.

And yet Reno's mind kept returning to Cade. He'd ridden with her all evening, genuinely upset that Plenty Coups and the mares were missing. He wasn't just concerned about the mustangs his organization was sworn to protect.

After an hour on the telephone, Reno felt her eyes growing heavy. She'd make more calls tomorrow. She barely summoned the energy to climb the stairs to her room, but taking a shower refreshed her. She slipped on a clean pair of jeans and a T-shirt, and went back downstairs.

Wynonna was sitting on the couch in her nightgown. Reno glanced at the clock on the mantel. Almost eleven. Where had the day gone?

"I'm going to bed," Wy said, rising. "You should get some rest, too, Reno."

"I know." But in spite of her weariness, she was wide-awake. "I'll turn in shortly. Think I'll get a little air first." Taking a cold Mountain Dew from the refrigerator, she walked out onto the porch, where the dogs were lounging.

Kicking back in one of the chairs, she placed her bare feet on the railing. Immediately Tank began to growl. Tensing, Reno set her feet back down on the porch and stood. Her eyes had already adjusted to the darkness, and she spotted Cade as he walked up the driveway.

Tank and Willow dived off the porch, Blue Dog one step ahead of them, while Snap barked from the steps, hackles raised. Reno called the dogs back, and Cade paused.

"What are you doing here at this hour?" She narrowed her eyes, able to make out his face as he stepped into range of the porch light.

"I needed to talk to you."

"We talked all day."

"I mean without anyone else around." He eyed the dogs. "Can I come up?"

No. "I guess." After all, he'd ridden hard today, helping to hunt down her horses and the poachers.

His boot heels clicked against the wooden steps, and he paused to give Snap a pat on the head. "I wasn't sure you'd still be up," he said. "I parked down the driveway so I wouldn't wake anyone if the lights were off." He gave Tank a tentative rub. "Guess it wouldn't have mattered much, once these fellas saw me."

"They're all females, except him."

"Oh. I guess you don't have Sage and Sable anymore."

Her grandfather's dogs had lived only slightly longer than Grandpa Mel had.

"No." The thought that Cade had been gone long enough for the two German shepherds to grow old and die only emphasized the passage of time, filling Reno with an odd sadness.

Tank sniffed Cade's hand, then wagged his snow-white tail, willing to be friends on Reno's okay. "How'd the poachers manage to get to your horses with these dogs on guard?"

"I don't think they did it easily. The dogs were pretty agitated when I found them out by the paddock. Blue Dog had been running in the brush." She sat back down, rubbing the Catahoula's back with her bare toes. "Austin's going to check with the hospital for anyone who might've come in with a dog bite."

"Good idea." Crossing his ankles, Cade leaned against the porch railing, and Reno was rendered half-stupid by the sight of him in the moonlight.

Cowboy hat, faded jeans, scuffed boots…he'd never looked better.

"Did you check the latch on your paddock gate?"

"It isn't broken, if that's what you're thinking."

"I was kind of hoping it was," Cade said. "That maybe Plenty Coups and the mares had wandered off."

Reno wished the same. But even if one of the horses had managed to work the latch open with its mouth—a trick more than one of her horses had

been able to do in the past—they would've come
back to the barn by now. They were used to getting
sweet feed every morning and evening, and unless
they'd gone clear down to the river, they'd be thirsty
enough to return to the water tanks out back, if
nothing else.

"Cade, you didn't come here to talk to me about
my gate latch."

"No." He took a deep breath. "I guess I came to
give you a long-overdue apology."

"That right?"

"I was wrong to leave all those years ago, Reno.
I'm more sorry than you'll ever know, and I'm
sorry that I had to kill Sonny…. Sorry for what
happened to your mom."

Reno refused to let his words touch her. *Too
little, too late.* "Why are you trying so hard to make
up for the past, Cade?"

"I don't know what you mean."

"I understand you're a BLM agent in Idaho, but
there's no reason for you to work so hard to help
Sam Grainger here. Unless, of course, you're trying
to make things up to me and maybe to my grandfather by stopping the poachers."

"I hardly think saving your mustangs will right
the wrongs I've done, Reno." He'd said it quietly,
but his face was red, and she knew he wasn't being
completely truthful. "I…" He gestured aimlessly,
then let his hand fall. "Yeah, I want to help Sam

help you, because I know what those mustangs mean to you and what they meant to your grandfather. And yes, I hate that I hurt you years ago. Damn it, Reno, I came over here to try to explain why I left."

"I'm listening." She folded her arms, staring up at him, teeth clenched.

"I ran because I couldn't deal with taking the life of another human being, no matter how awful the guy was. Some people believe in the death penalty. I'm not one of them."

"Well, I am," Reno said. "And I'd say Sonny got what he deserved. So why the hell did his death upset you so much? He was *my* father, Cade. *My* stepfather." She fought to keep her voice from quivering. "You should've been there for me, Cade. Period."

"I know that. But I couldn't stay. Even as a lawman, who was I to decide whether or not to take a life? That's up to God."

"Yeah, and God was looking after you when you pulled that trigger before Sonny could pull his a second time. Isn't that what being a cop is all about? To serve and to protect?"

"That's just it." Cade collapsed into the chair beside Reno, staring intently at her. "I hadn't been able to do a damn thing to protect those young girls from what was going on right under my nose. Do you know how many times I questioned whether Sonny had molested you, even though you denied it?"

"He didn't."

But he'd come close.

Reno felt cold.

"All I could do was try to stop Sonny after the fact, by arresting him and sending him to prison. Instead, he holed up in that shack…."

"You had no alternative, Cade. Unless you would've chosen to give up your own life instead."

"Exactly. I had only one choice, and I took it. But then I had to live with it. Some days I'm not so sure I can."

"He would've killed you."

"I know that. But knowing it has never helped me sleep at night. To top it off, my thoughts were all jumbled up with how I felt about you. What Sonny did made me so sick, I couldn't fathom having feelings for someone who was little more than a kid. I felt so old, Reno. So much older than twenty-five. But I was truly just a kid myself. I couldn't face you. Your grandpa was right—I was a coward." He swallowed. "I came back to help Mom and Dad, but I'm also here to make amends to you, Reno."

"For what? For saving me from Sonny before he went too far? Or from the trial that would've had me and Mom the talk of the gossip mill for months?"

He blanched. "I never thought about what a trial would've done to you."

"Well, maybe you'd better go home and think about it."

"It doesn't matter, Reno. I might be able to live with putting Sonny six feet under, but I'll never forgive myself that it caused your mother to take her life."

"Why are you here?" Reno repeated. She bit the inside of her cheek.

"I still care about you, Reno. But I don't ever want to hurt you again. I'll be going back to Idaho after Dad…"

"I understand that." She gave a dry laugh. "Cade, everyone I've ever cared about has left me, one way or another, except Wynonna. I'm afraid I don't trust anyone anymore. So you see, you're here preaching to the choir." She raised her hands, palms up. "I've already told myself I'll never let you hurt me again. I feel nothing for you, Cade. Not contempt, not love…nothing."

Liar.

She could forgive him for leaving, but she couldn't forget.

"Gee, Reno, why don't you tell me how you really feel?" Cade stood. "Even if my life wasn't in Idaho, I could never be with you."

"We're all grown up now, Cade. Don't tell me you still think a seven-year age difference matters."

"No, it doesn't. But what does matter is I can't forget any more than you can. I can't stay around you and see pain in your eyes. You don't realize it, but it's there. You miss your mom."

Reno swallowed. *Of course she did.*

"Let's face it," Cade continued, "your mom would still be here if the shooting hadn't happened, and maybe even your grandfather. Maybe Mel wouldn't have had a stroke if he wasn't under so much stress."

Her ears rang, knowing she'd thought the same thing.

She didn't want to think about it now.

"You're sure full of yourself, Mr. BLM Agent."

He scowled at her. "All I'm saying is I can't forget the good times, either. Good times you and I had, and good times you had with Sonny and your mother as a family. He used to take you fishing…and swimming. God, Reno, that's what's been the hardest thing of all. To equate the man I thought your dad was with the monster he turned out to be."

Reno stood and paced. "I think about stuff like that, too, you know," she said. "Sonny treated me kindly, yes. And he seemed to make Mom happy. But you know what else? Looking back on it, I can remember a time or two when he made an inappropriate comment to me when Mom wasn't around. Or laid his hand on my knee for just a little too long."

Cade froze. "I didn't know that."

"She saw what she wanted to," Reno said, pain she'd buried making her nauseous. Quickly she added, "Sonny never took it any further. He knew my grandfather would kill him if he did."

"I would've, too." The words were out before Cade realized what he'd said.

"That's right," Reno said. "So put it behind you, Cade. Take care of your father."

He stood. "I will. But I want to help Sam catch the poachers, and get Plenty Coups and your mares back."

"I appreciate that, Cade. I really do. But you have to stop worrying about me and what's in the past, and focus on your family. Your parents need you, and your mother will need you even more if something happens to your dad." Reno frowned. "Who's taking care of your place in Idaho while you're away?"

"I leased it out. I'm not sure how long I'll be staying here, but I figured it would be awhile, anyway."

Suddenly Reno felt terrible for being so hard on him. How awful for Cade, to have to think about waiting for his dad to get worse and die, or…what? She prayed for a miracle that would let the old cowboy be around for as long as possible. She liked Matt.

"Cade, if there's anything I can do to help, let

me know," she said impulsively. "Your mom mentioned moving your cows to better pasture. I've moved cows before."

"To say the least," Cade growled. She and Grandpa Mel had moved a lot of cows, and even more horses. "I know bringing in a herd of horses takes more riding skill, and actually, I *could* use some help tomorrow. Mom doesn't like to leave Dad all alone, so Heath and I will be moving three hundred head. They broke through the fence this evening and drifted down by the barn. We need to run them back up into the high country."

Reno had wanted to look for signs of her missing horses tomorrow, but with Cade working hard to help her, she could hardly refuse him.

"I'll be there. What time?"

"About seven-thirty. I need to feed first, and patch the fence."

"Okay."

He didn't take his eyes off her, and Reno grew uncomfortable.

"Come here," he said.

Before she knew what was happening, Cade reached out and took hold of her elbow, pulling her close. His bear hug caught her off guard. She didn't remember him holding her that way in…forever. She could barely breathe when he buried his face in her hair, and the kiss he pressed on top of her head left her trembling.

He let go abruptly. "I'd better leave so you can get some sleep. You'll need to be rested if you're going to help me tomorrow."

"Right."

"Just make sure your dogs don't eat me up before I get to my truck." He turned and took the steps two at a time, then glanced back over his shoulder. "See you tomorrow."

CHAPTER SEVEN

CADE WAS OUT like a snuffed candle the minute his head hit the pillow. Unfortunately, he woke right back up again and lay awake the better part of the night. But it wasn't the poachers robbing him of sleep. It was the same old nightmare….

He could clearly see the dilapidated house, tucked amidst the trees, where Sonny Sanchez had holed up. Then suddenly mist swirled across the gray sky, momentarily marring his vision. Gun drawn, he crept along the narrow game trail that wound around behind the abandoned house. His footsteps seemed unnaturally loud in the stillness.

"Come out, Sanchez!" he ordered. "We've got you surrounded."

From the house he heard sobbing…a child's voice.

"Sanchez!" he shouted.

But it wasn't Sonny who opened the front door. A little girl stepped outside, a girl who somehow was Reno. She held her little arms high in the air.

"Don't," she said, shaking her head. Tears streamed down her cheeks. "Please don't shoot my daddy."

"It's too late." Cade held his pistol aloft, away from the child. "You have to move out of the way. Get back where you're safe!"

In the living room window he saw Sonny, staring through ragged curtains. A wicked grin split his features, and as Cade stood watching, Sanchez began to laugh.

"You can't stop me," he said. "I'll keep doing it…keep hurting little girls. Big girls, too."

"Cade, don't."

He snapped his gaze around to the child, and her image shimmered, faded, and became a grown Reno. She stood there, hands outstretched, eyes pleading. "Don't shoot my dad."

"I have to." Cade faced the window once more. "Stop laughing," he shouted at Sanchez. "Stop it."

"I can't stop." Sonny shook his head, still grinning. "I'll never stop."

The pistol bucked in his hand as Cade fired. His limbs felt heavy, but he gripped the gun with both hands and fired again. Sonny's expression froze, stunned for a moment as blood spread across his chest, staining the white shirt he wore. Then a bone-chilling look of satisfaction spread across his face. He'd gotten what he'd wanted—suicide by cop. Mist swirled again over the yard, and suddenly

Sonny was standing on the walkway outside the house.

"Help him."

Cade turned to see Reno standing nearby.

"Look what you've done." Reno knelt beside her stepdad as he fell to the ground. Reno cradled his head in her lap, and her face shifted and changed until she was no longer Reno.

Instead, Carlina Sanchez knelt on the blood-soaked ground, her dying husband's head cradled in her lap. Her skirt became soaked with blood. "He didn't mean it. He didn't mean to hurt anyone." She stared helplessly at Cade. "What will I do now? What will I do?"

Cade had awakened with a jerk, sitting straight up in bed. In reality, neither Reno nor her mother had witnessed the shooting, only his fellow lawmen. But they might as well have. He'd never been able to shake the feeling of having blood on his hands. And he'd sure never meant to hurt Reno....

The sweet scent of her hair last night as they'd stood on her porch, the warmth of her supple body in his arms…it had taken every ounce of his control to keep from kissing her, to settle for brushing his lips against her hair. Then let go of her and walk away.

And now, hours later, he could barely focus enough to saddle his horse, knowing Reno would be here any minute. What had he been thinking, asking her to ride with him? With his dad's two cow dogs, he and Heath probably could've handled the herd by themselves.

The sound of a truck rattling up the driveway broke into his thoughts. Cade looked up from tightening his cinch to see Reno pulling in. His dad's red heelers trotted over, tails wagging as she got out of her pickup. She gave him a wave, then went straight back and unloaded the white mustang she called Cloud. The mare laid her ears back as the heelers got nosy, sniffing her hind hooves.

"Sierra! Sadie!" Cade called. The dogs immediately dropped back to the hitching post. Sadie heeled one of the barn cats before dropping down in the dirt beside Sierra.

Estelle came from the stables with Heath, who was leading his strawberry roan gelding. "I can't thank you enough for helping out," she said to Reno. "I'd do it, but I hate to leave Matt alone."

"No problem," Reno exclaimed.

Cade's mom turned toward him. "Your father won't even come outside. I thought I might at least talk him into getting some fresh air. You were right to take him for a drive to Reno's that day. Maybe I have been overprotective." Her eyes filled with sadness. "He loves being on a horse. I wish he'd still take a pleasure ride now and then."

"You know he won't," Cade said. Pushing cows

was the ranch chore his father had always enjoyed most, that and riding fence. There was something about working together as a team, enjoying the beauty of the outdoors, that had bonded Cade to his dad at an early age. As a kid, he'd felt so important, hammering a fence staple. Pulling a wire tight, with help from his dad....

"Reno, I'm so sorry about your horses," his mom was saying, and the two women chatted while Cade ran a hoof pick over Jet's feet. He liked to be sure his mount was in top shape before they started out, and he'd clean the gelding's hooves again once they got back. They'd be covering some rocky ground.

Reno seemed to avoid looking directly at him, and Cade wondered if she was sorry she'd agreed to come over.

Once Heath had the roan saddled, the three set off through the bottom pastureland behind the barn. The cows were scattered among the scrub oak and piñon junipers, along with their half-grown calves. Gathering them would take some time.

Cade had already repaired the downed fence, so they'd be moving the herd toward a gate not far from where they'd gone through the wire. Too bad the silly things hadn't waited until next month to help themselves to the bottomland. Cade would be bringing them down from the high country then, but for now the lower pasture needed a rest for the grass to grow back.

Heath took the left side once they finally had the cattle together. Reno rode drag with Cade, bringing up the rear, directing the dogs toward the strays and stragglers. The ground rose and fell in a series of gullies as they climbed, growing rougher the higher they moved. But the heelers knew their job, and things went more smoothly than he'd expected. Until a coyote popped out of the brush on the hillside above.

Startled by the sight of the dogs and the moving herd, the animal quickly put distance between itself and the sound of human voices. But Cloud had been walking the ridge mere yards from where the coyote made its appearance. Reno had gone after a cow and calf that had broken from the herd, and as she drove the animals back to the group, her mare perked her ears at the sight of the predator.

Reno corrected Cloud with a nudge of one spur, letting her know where her attention ought to be, but the stubborn mustang rebelled. Pinning her ears back, she humped her spine and began to buck in earnest.

Reno sat tight in the saddle, and Cade watched her ride with the same admiration he'd felt years ago. He had no doubt she would line the mare out in a hurry. But he hadn't factored in the steep terrain.

Cloud bucked, then misstepped, her right hind leg slipping down the nearly vertical slope. She

scrambled to keep her balance, but her wild antics
had cost her her footing. The mare fell, with Reno
still in the saddle, and Cade let out a warning
shout—too late. The gray rolled backward, and disappeared into the gully.

Dear God!

Heart in his throat, Cade spurred Jet toward
the top of the rim. He pictured Reno lying crushed
and broken beneath the big mustang's body. But
when he reached the rise and looked down, Cloud
was scrambling to her feet, miraculously
unharmed, though the saddle tilted at a crazy
angle. She shook herself like a big dog, then
trotted on to merge with the cows, which promptly
spooked and scattered.

Cade called to Heath, who chased after the mare,
while he himself hustled Jet down the gully to
where Reno lay, flat on her back. He was out of the
saddle and beside her in an instant.

"Reno. Can you hear me?"

She stared at him, but made no effort to move—
or make a sound. The panic in her eyes told him
she'd had the wind knocked out of her. He knew the
awful feeling of not being able to breathe in or out.

"You've got the wind knocked out of you. Just
lie still." He wanted to cradle her head, but was
afraid to move her in case her injuries were more
serious than he thought.

Reno managed a nod, then grasped her left wrist.

Cade didn't like the way it looked. The unnatural angle told him it was likely broken.

Heath appeared beside him a moment later, ponying Cloud alongside his strawberry roan. "Is she all right?"

By now, Reno had finally gotten her breath. Nodding, she greedily sucked in air. "Yeah," she managed to croak. "I think." But she groaned. "My arm doesn't feel so good."

Gently, Cade probed the area above her wrist, and Reno winced, biting back a yelp. "You've broken it," he said. "Damn, this is my fault."

"How do you figure that?" Reno glared at him, trying to sit up. "Where's my hat?"

He got it for her, placing it on her head as he helped her into a sitting position. "I shouldn't have asked you to come out here. We could've managed without you."

"Now you tell me." She winced again, then glared at him, hugging her bad arm. "Don't be ridiculous. You think this is the first time I've been hurt riding horses?"

"Why, Reno, I didn't think you'd ever been bucked off before," Cade said, in an effort to keep her mind off her pain. "Shoot, why do you think I quit rodeo when I did? I was afraid you were getting good enough to show me up if you decided to take up bronc riding for sport."

Her dark eyes softened and Cade realized then

that the feelings he'd harbored for Reno had never died. He'd tried to kill them off in every way he could think of, including putting almost nine hundred miles between the two of them. But now, as he gazed at her, the sound of the lowing cows faded to the background. He wanted to kiss her hurt and make it go away. All of it.

"Heath can't gather the cows alone," Reno said, her face pinched, her expression determined.

"Reno, I—" Heath started.

"It's okay. Go on and help him, Cade. I've been hurt worse than this." With Cade's assistance, she stood and reached for Cloud's reins. Heath had righted her saddle.

"You can't ride with a broken arm," Cade protested.

"My arm's broken, not my leg," she grunted. "Besides, it's better than walking out of here. Definitely faster. Unless you have a helicopter back at the Diamond L I don't know about."

Cade pursed his lips. "You're stubborn as hell, you know that?"

Reno winced, then smiled briefly. "So I've been told." Gripping the one-piece roping rein of Cloud's bridle with her good hand, she mounted the mare from the off side, making another face as her butt hit the saddle.

"You sure you want to ride Cloud back? You can double with me."

"Fall off, get back on," she said.

He knew it wouldn't do to keep arguing with her. "All right then." He swung back into the saddle. "But the cows can wait."

Stubborn cowgirl.

He hid a smile. It was one of the things he loved most about Reno.

BY THE TIME RENO LEFT the hospital room with a cast on her arm, she was more than ready to go home. She'd broken her wrist in two places, and had spent over three hours in the waiting room, exam room and X-ray unit.

"Three hours?" she muttered for the umpteenth time as they drove along in Cade's truck. She looked at him through a haze from the shot of Demerol she'd been given. Her head felt as if it were going to float right off her shoulders. She'd refused the medication at first, thinking she could do without it. But as time passed, the pain became unbearable, and Reno had finally given in. "A person could die waiting to be taken care of in that freaking hospital."

Cade grunted. "Tell me about it."

"Guess you've been there once or twice yourself, bronc rider." She frowned. "Hey, where're you going?"

"To your place." His tone indicated that should be obvious.

"What about Cloud?" Cade had unsaddled the mustang back at the Diamond L, and turned her out in the round pen with Jet.

"What about her? She'll be fine. I'll haul her back to your place later."

"I could do it," Reno mumbled.

"Not on those painkillers," Cade said. In addition to the shot, the E.R. doctor had sent Reno home with a sample packet of acetaminophen with codeine, along with a prescription for more.

"Well…once it wears off."

"Trust me, when that shot wears off, you'll want a pill or two. And you won't want to be hauling horses."

They pulled down the private road that led to Reno's driveway, and as Cade swung in to park between the house and barn, she did a double take. Surely the shot hadn't fogged her brain *that* much.

Plenty Coups, Honey and the other two missing mares stood in the paddock outside the barn. "Cade!" Reno pointed.

"What the hell?" He got out and moved to help her from the truck, but she beat him to it, already making a beeline for the horses.

"Plenty Coups!" Reno ducked through the rail fence and wrapped her healthy arm around the gelding's neck. She patted and hugged him, then the mares, crooning words of affection. "Where have you been, baby?" She ran her hand over

Plenty Coups's black mane, pulling sticks and pieces of sagebrush out of it.

Reno watched as Cade walked over to the paddock gate to check the latch. A firm shake showed it was secure. He studied the rangeland around them, and the surrounding mountains, and she did the same, blinking heavily. Though she tried hard to focus, she didn't see movement anywhere.

When she and Cade had pulled in, the dogs had trotted down the driveway to greet them, all but Willow, and now Reno looked down to find the German shepherd brushing against her leg. The dog had something in her mouth, which she dropped at Reno's feet before looking up with expressive eyes. She loved to play fetch.

Reno bent to examine the object.

"What's that?" Cade asked, returning from the gate.

"A bone." It wasn't unusual for the dogs to drag home a piece of deer or elk left behind by predators or hunters. But this was no natural bone. "One of those smoked kind you can buy at the pet supply." She turned the large knucklebone over in her hand. It looked new, and teeth marks indicated Willow had been enjoying it immensely. Nearly all the sinew and likely the barbecue flavoring had been chewed away. "I don't buy these for my dogs. I only give them rawhide chews."

"Where would she have found it then?"

"Beats me."

"Well, someone had to have given it to her. Would Wynonna?"

"Uh-uh. So…someone brings back my horses, maybe gives the dogs a treat to distract them? If poachers took the horses, it makes no sense that they would return them."

"Are you sure the mustangs didn't just get out in the first place?" Cade asked. "Maybe a neighbor found them and brought them back."

Reno struggled to stay alert. She needed to go lie down. "No. I told you the gate was closed and latched. I'm sure of it." She also reminded him of the hoofprints and boot prints she'd found. "Do you think someone tried to poison my dogs?" Willow whined, wanting her prize back. Reno gave it a tentative sniff, but smelled only doggy breath and faint hickory smoke.

"I doubt they'd use a bone," Cade said. "And besides, they would've done it before now."

"True." Still worried, Reno checked Willow over carefully, then called the other three dogs. They all seemed fine.

"Look here," Cade said, searching around the paddock.

Reno saw the fresh tracks of shod hoofprints. A few feet from the paddock, Reno spotted another knucklebone, lying near the brush.

"I'd say someone did use these treats to distract your dogs," Cade said, "while they put your horses back."

Reno rubbed her temple, willing her mind to clear. "This isn't making any sense. Who would do that, instead of just calling me, you or the sheriff's office?"

"Beats me." Cade wrapped his arm around her shoulder. "Come on, you're in no shape to be out here. You have to go sleep off that painkiller and rest your arm." Gently, he guided her toward the house. "How's it feeling?"

"It's still throbbing, believe it or not."

"Even more reason to rest."

"I can't rest," Reno protested. "I have to take care of my animals."

"I'll do it."

"You've already got enough on your plate. And your mom and Heath need you. Cloud scattered your herd."

"At least let me walk you to the house. Looks like Wynonna is home."

Wy's truck was in the driveway, and the house-keeper came hurrying forward as Cade helped Reno up the steps.

"Oh my gosh, what happened?" Wynonna clutched a hand to her breast, then reached for her.

"I'm okay. Took a spill, that's all."

She stared pointedly at the neon-green cast on Reno's arm. "Looks like more than a 'spill.'"

Cade filled her in on what had happened. "Is

there someone to help you with the chores, Wy-nonna? Reno's about to crash."

She nodded. "I'll call one of our volunteers. As a matter of fact, Maura McPherson seemed pretty interested in helping out when we talked to her yesterday at the barbecue."

"She gave me her phone number," Reno said. "It's on my desk."

"Perfect. I'll call her, and Shelly, too." Heath's sister, Shelly, was their primary volunteer.

"Thanks, Wy." Reno tried to shrug away from Cade's grasp, but he didn't let go. His hand felt warm and strong on her upper arm, yet gentle. Was it his touch causing the tingly feeling that was working its way through her body, or the Demerol? *Oh, my.* He'd slipped his arm around her waist.

"You need to lie down," Cade repeated. "Prop your wrist up. Want me to take you to your room?"

Now there was a loaded question.

Had to be the drugs making her think this way.

"The couch is okay," Reno mumbled. "Gotta sleep. Find out who brought back my horses."

"What's she babbling about?" Wy's voice seemed to be coming from a distance as she placed a pillow under Reno's head and another under her arm, while Cade covered her with the afghan that was normally draped over the back of the couch.

"Plenty Coups and the mares are in the paddock," he answered.

"What? But I didn't hear..." Wynonna fussed with the pillow, making sure Reno's wrist was properly elevated. "Truthfully, I haven't been home long. I went to the crafts store."

"Did you see any strange rigs around here? Horseback riders, anything?" Cade asked.

"No, I didn't."

"I've got to leave for a while," Cade said next. Was that reluctance in his voice? *Drugs again.* "But I'll be back as soon as I can."

"Should I call the sheriff?" Wynonna asked.

"If you would," Cade said. "Take it easy for a while, stubborn."

Reno barely heard him walk away as she slipped into a deep sleep.

CHAPTER EIGHT

BY THE TIME he and Heath got the cows gathered, Cade was tired, but still thinking about Reno and her horses. Who in the world had brought them back, and why? Had the poachers decided Plenty Coups and his dam were too recognizable? None of the horses were freeze branded. Maybe Reno ought to consider doing that as further precaution. Her grandpa had always been against horse branding of any kind, though he'd reluctantly registered a brand and marked his cattle.

If cows got out and mixed together with a neighbor's herd, it could be tedious sorting them without a brand. It was a lot easier to identify individual horses.

A hot shower relieved some of the soreness in Cade's muscles. He dressed and went back downstairs to the kitchen, where his parents were waiting. Matt was reading the paper, and country music played on the radio.

"I feel so bad about what happened to Reno,"

Estelle said. "I should've been out there helping you instead of asking her to do it."

"You could've been," her husband said, "if you weren't so busy hovering over me all the time."

Estelle ignored him.

"You didn't ask her, I did," Cade stated.

"Well, anyway, I made some muffins for Reno and Wynonna." She indicated a covered basket sitting on the table. "If you go over to check on her, will you take them?"

Cade nodded. "I'm going over right now. You don't have to hold supper for me—I'll grab a bite at the diner." He kissed her on the cheek. "See you later, Mom. Bye, Dad."

"Tell Reno to feel better," Matt called.

A short time later, Cade arrived at Reno's and noted a Chevy S-10 parked behind Reno's old pickup, another car beside it. Company? He was relieved to see she had someone to help her, yet couldn't shake the notion that the someone should be him. No matter what Reno had said last night.

"Cade, come on in," Wynonna said, after opening the door. "Reno is sleeping."

"Still?"

"She woke up once, took a pain pill, which I practically had to shove down her throat, then went back to sleep. I couldn't get her to eat anything, but Maura's here to help with the horses.

Heath's sister just got off her shift at the vet's office, as well. She's Dr. Russell's receptionist."

"Maybe these will whet Reno's appetite." Cade handed over the basket of muffins.

The scent of cinnamon and apple wafted out as Wynonna pulled the cloth back to admire the home-baked treat. "How nice of your mother. You can go on into the living room. Maura and Shelly are out in the barn. I'm sure Reno will want to see you."

"I don't want to wake her."

"No worries. She's sleeping like the dead, but she'll probably wake up again soon. Meanwhile, I'll get you something to drink."

In the living room, Cade watched Reno sleep. She reminded him of one of her mustangs—strong, tough, magnificent. As though sensing his presence, she began to stir.

"What's wrong?" she asked, blinking.

"Does something have to be wrong for me to pay a visit to a friend?" His tongue felt thick as he said the words. He wanted more than friend-ship from her.

"What time is it?" Reno turned to look at the clock on the DVD player, and groaned. "I can't believe I slept so long. Are Shelly and Maura still here?"

"They're feeding."

"I feel guilty lying here like this." Reposition-ing her arm on the pillow as she sat up, she used her other hand to work the band out of her hair, then raked her fingers through it as it fell down her back.

Cade nearly swallowed his tongue.

"So, what's up?"

"Nothing new. Like I said, I came out here to see how you were doing."

"I can't sit here any longer," Reno announced suddenly, even though she looked a little out of it. "I'm going to check on Plenty Coups and the mares." Awkwardly, she pulled on her boots, and he moved to help her, knowing there would be no use arguing with her to stay put and rest.

"Maybe you ought to put them in the barn. I'll do it for you," he added, seeing that she was already prepared to ignore her injury. "Besides, I brought my farrier tools. I'll replace Plenty Coups's shoe."

For once, Reno didn't protest. Her pinched face told him she was in pain, in spite of the medication. She'd taken a pretty rough spill.

Plenty Coups nickered when he spotted Reno. She hurried to the horse, pressing her face against his nose as he nuzzled her. With her free hand, she stroked the star on his forehead, murmuring to him, then to Honey and the other mares. "I'll get their halters," she finally said.

Cade followed her to the barn, where Maura was loading a bale of hay onto a wheelbarrow.

"Hi, Reno. Cade," she called. "Shelly and I have just about gotten everybody fed, even the dogs."

She motioned toward Reno's cast. "How's your wrist feeling? Wy said you took one heck of a fall."

"It'll feel better once it quits hurting," Reno said.

Maura grinned. "I'd better get back to work. Thanks for letting me help with the horses. I'm loving it."

"Don't be silly," Reno said. "I owe you big-time for doing my chores. Feel free to go riding, by the way, anytime you want—though I wouldn't recommend Cloud."

Maura laughed again. "I'll remember that. Shelly's out watering the rescue horses."

"Would you mind getting stalls ready for Plenty Coups and the mares? I'm going to put them in the barn for the night."

"Not at all. The stalls are clean. I'll just toss some hay in and check the water."

"Have you considered locking up all of your horses?" Cade asked.

"I don't have enough room," Reno said. "Most of them stay out on pasture or in paddocks, with three-sided shelters." Her brow furrowed. "Why would the poachers try to steal my horses again, if they already brought them back?"

"Who says they brought them back? Maybe someone else did."

"That doesn't make any sense," Reno said.

"Well, I don't know what to make of it," Cade replied, adjusting his hat. "It's odd, that's for sure.

But you can't be sure the poachers won't come back for some of your other horses, maybe some that aren't as recognizable." Plenty Coups and the three mustang mares were all stand-out colors— blue roan, red dun, two loud Appaloosas. "And if they do, what's to stop them?"

"My twelve-gauge shotgun."

"You can't shoot it," Cade said pointedly, indicating her cast.

"Okay, then. My .38." She smiled sweetly. "I can also get more of my volunteers out here whenever they have free time. Maybe having more people around will dissuade any thieves."

"I've got a small camp trailer," Maura offered. "I can park it out by the paddocks, and Shelly and I could sleep there."

"I don't think that's wise," Cade said. "I wouldn't want to see you in harm's way."

"Well, we have to do something," Reno said. "Not that I want you or Shelly to do anything that will get you hurt, Maura. Why did I have to go and break my arm now?"

"It's not as if you planned it," Cade said. He took the nylon halters from her, and the two walked outside. Cade caught the gelding, but Reno stubbornly insisted on leading him.

"I can walk him with one hand."

"Fine."

She led the roan to Cade's pickup truck, and

held the gelding's lead rope while Cade set up his anvil on the tailgate. In short order, he'd replaced the missing shoe and checked the other three.

Back at the barn, Maura was gone, but she'd readied the box stalls as promised. Cade put the horses in, then hung their halters on hooks outside the stall doors.

"Cade, I truly appreciate all you're doing for me, for the mustangs, but…" Reno lowered her gaze. "Remember what we talked about last night?"

He could hardly forget.

"Taking care of an injured cowgirl isn't your job."

"You broke your arm helping me. I'm returning the favor." But he knew there was more to it than that. He liked spending time with Reno.

Again, he wished there was some way to change the past.

RENO'S WRIST THROBBED mercilessly, and she knew she should go back inside and lie down, but she couldn't. It bothered the hell out of her to be dependent on someone else. She didn't want Cade taking care of her.

But she was also starting to like having him around. Today, the simple act of watching him shoe Plenty Coups felt like old times.

"Have you had supper?" she found herself asking.

"I planned to eat at the diner."

"There's no need for that, when Wynonna's bound to have something cooking on the stove. She'll have my hide if I let you leave without eating."

"Guess I don't want that." He grinned crookedly, making Reno's blood pressure rise.

He walked with her to the house and opened the door for her. But the minute they reached the kitchen, Wynonna held out a picnic basket.

"Since I know you won't listen to the doctor and rest your arm," Wy said, her dark eyes stern, "you might as well get some fresh air. It will make you sleep tonight, and maybe you won't need your pain pills. So here's a picnic supper for you both. Enjoy."

"But—" Reno started to protest.

"Go on." Wynonna waved them away. "Shelly and Maura will eat with me."

"Okay." Reno shrugged. She didn't want to hurt Wy's feelings, or be rude to Cade, after his helpfulness.

"Thanks, Wynonna," he said, taking the basket.

"Where should we eat?" Reno asked as she stepped back out onto the porch with him.

"It's your land. Where's a nice spot?"

As soon as the words were out, Reno knew she and Cade had the same thought. They knew a spot, all right. One where they'd picnicked as kids. They'd last been there the year before everything fell apart.

"Not there," Reno said.

"Okay." He didn't even try to pretend he didn't know what she meant.

"On second thought, let's do go there." She was through with hiding from her feelings. "It's a nice place to picnic, and we're not kids anymore, right?"

"Right." Cade lifted a shoulder. "I'll drive." There was a back road that led to their old picnic spot—if you could call it a road. More like a trail for four-wheel drives.

"The shortcut on horseback is better," Reno said. Riding in his truck would feel too much like a date. This was merely an outing for two old friends. Two people trying to put the past to rest. "We can trade the basket for saddlebags."

The look he gave her said it all.

"What?" She raised her eyebrows. "I can ride, if you'll help me saddle Plenty Coups. You can ride Honey."

"Reno, that's the happy pills talking. You might reinjure your arm."

"I won't. Come on, cowboy. Unless you'd rather I try to saddle my roan by myself?" She smiled inwardly at the sigh she heard behind her as she set off for the barn, and could picture the eye roll that went with it.

Her challenge was no more than a bluff. Her wrist hurt too badly to use it for anything, still she wanted to ride. The E.R. doctor had told her the cast would stay on for six weeks, and after that, light weight lifting would help her build the muscle back up, and also strengthen her grip. At the moment, she could barely close her fingers.

The shortcut took just twenty-five minutes, through sagebrush and trees, over the gently sloping mountain to the east of the ranch house.

Reno kept her eyes open for any sign of mustangs. The poachers couldn't have gotten away with all of them. The herd was too large. Unless, of course, they'd used more than the one rig spotted in town. She was still sick over the loss of Storm-Bringer. It wasn't fair. Damned poachers.

"Look," Cade said a moment later. "Tracks, unshod."

Sure enough, the mustangs had passed through here recently, fresh manure confirming the fact. "They're probably confused, looking for their missing band members," Reno said. "I wonder if Windchaser, the stallion, is still with them?"

Or if the bachelor band was still intact. The smaller herd was made up of colts too old to be accepted by the stallion anymore—two- and three-year-olds, and some long yearlings. As they grew older, they would try to steal mares from Windchaser or fight him for leadership of the main herd.

"I guess time will tell," Cade said. "I'm going to camp out with Sam as much as possible, since Paul is pulling double duty in De Beque."

Reno nodded. "I could—"

"No," he said firmly. "You're already hurt, and you've been shot at. That's enough of that."

She scowled, but said nothing. He had a point. Still, she couldn't sit idle. For the moment, as she and Cade reached their destination, she decided to relax and enjoy the picnic supper Wynonna had packed. Clutching her injured arm against her middle, Reno dismounted and stood for a moment, reins in her good hand, simply admiring the view.

They stood on the edge of a small, hidden canyon. Rocky crags lined the rim above the sheer walls, where a few piñon junipers clung precariously. It was a spot Reno had once visited often. A spot she'd been unable to return to after Cade left.

She reached to untie the blanket she'd secured to the cantle of her saddle. *Damn.* She kept forgetting she had only one usable hand, until her wrist throbbed.

"I'll get that." Cade took the blanket, and Reno watched as he spread it on the ground, then laid out their meal.

Suddenly her throat closed, and she wasn't sure she could eat. The last time she'd picnicked with him here, she'd been a kid with conflicting emotions. Nearly eighteen, she'd begun to develop a crush on him.

One she knew he didn't return. So she'd fought it, happy to have him in her life at all.

And then he'd left.

Get over it. She was okay. She and Cade had hashed everything out on her porch last night. There was no reason they couldn't be friends.

"Looks fantastic," Reno said, forcing herself to think about the food. It wasn't hard—her stomach was growling. She hadn't eaten since early this morning, before going to the Diamond L to help Cade gather the cows. It was now more than twelve hours later.

"If I lived with Wynonna, I'd weigh a ton," Cade said, unpacking containers of Indian fry bread, chicken, potato salad and chocolate cake. "I'd forgotten what a good cook she is until she brought all that stuff to the barbecue."

"Why do you think I have to keep so active?"

They fell silent, enjoying the meal. Wy had even packed a thermos of iced tea. Reno did her best to ignore the fact that Cade sat a little too close to her. They faced out over the canyon as the evening sun's slanting rays climbed the red rocks. In the distance, the mountains lit up with alpenglow—a deep shade of purple, rich and breathtaking.

"Check that—"

"Isn't that—"

She returned Cade's smile as they faced each other. "You go first," he said.

"I was thinking—" how handsome he was? "—that the mountains look phenomenal."

"Yeah." But he was no longer studying the view, and as Reno caught her breath, he inched even closer, then leaned in to kiss her.

Her initial impulse was to push him away. Instead, she found herself taking his mouth willingly, hungrily. Their tongues met, setting her on fire, burning brighter than the alpenglow. Reno moaned.

Slowly, Cade moved his hands to the small of her back, and the next thing she knew, he'd lowered her to the blanket. Lying above her, one leg draped over hers, he continued to kiss her senseless. And she let him. Until suddenly, hot tears were burning her eyes. She blinked them back and shoved him away with her good arm, struggling to sit up.

Startled, he helped her. "Reno, what's wrong? Did I hurt you?"

"You can't do this!" she said, emotion welling inside her. Feelings she'd held in check for years came out as she stared into those blue-green eyes that had driven her crazy all her life.

"What—? I only meant to kiss you, Reno. I wasn't—"

"Wasn't what? Going to try taking it to the next level? Or was it my heart you were planning to not get involved with?"

"Reno."

"No." Shaking her head, she stood. "I told you, I'm not going to let you hurt me again." She wiped

away the stupid tears running down her cheeks.
"Besides, I'm dating Austin." Even if he didn't set
her on fire the way Cade just had.

Cade looked as if she'd slapped him. "You're
right," he said quietly. "I'm sorry."

"We'd better go."

With that, she began to gather the remnants of
their meal, shoving empty containers and plastic
utensils into her saddlebags, not caring if her wrist
hurt as she used both hands.

"Reno, stop. Please." Cade touched her arm, and
she jerked away as though she'd been burned. She
had. Oh, she had. But that was all over. She was
done.

Swallowing back more tears, she embraced her
anger. It was an easier emotion to cope with. Exhausted, Reno threw the saddlebags over Plenty
Coups's back, and Cade retied the blanket to the
cantle. The fingers of her left hand felt numb, and
she knew she was being stupid, overdoing it.

Grudgingly, she let Cade remove the halters and
lead ropes they'd used to tie the horses, replacing
them with bridles. Cade looped the ropes into neat
coils, then hung them over the saddle horns. Holding her bad arm against her stomach, Reno gripped
the reins in her right hand and swung into the saddle.

With one final look at the canyon's beauty, she
rode away, knowing she'd be hard-pressed to ever
ride back to this spot again.

CHAPTER NINE

BIG MISTAKE, kissing Reno. At the Diamond L, Cade took a walk out back. He kicked viciously at a rock in his path, sending it flying against the barn wall. He was done. No more wasting time.

He spent the next several days helping Heath catch up on ranch chores. Sometimes he rode out with Sam over the mustangs' rangeland. The horses had returned to the water hole. Sam had been relieved to see only a few were missing—six or seven, as far as he could tell.

On a Tuesday, eight days after Reno had broken her wrist, Cade went to town. His cowboy boots were shot, and while breaking in a new pair would be a pain, literally, he needed them. There was a Western store, Ted's Tack and Feed, two miles out of town. Where Maura worked. Ted's hadn't been here nine years ago—Eagle's Nest had made do with the local co-op.

The building looked like a rustic log cabin, dark half logs stained to appear weathered with age. On the roof overlooking the parking lot stood a life-size statue of a buckskin quarter horse, the name of the place in faux barbed-wire lettering above it.

A bell tinkled when Cade opened the door, and he was immediately engulfed by the scents of new leather and sweet grain. His heels clicked against the polished hardwood floor as he strode toward the footwear section, passing a display of silver- and gold-plated belt buckles in a glass case to his left. A sign taped to it read "Quality German and sterling silver buckles, starting at $99.99."

Gotta love that one-cent saving.

Maura stepped out from behind the counter.

"Cade, how are you? Is there something I can help you with?"

"I need a good pair of boots."

"I think we can fix you up. What size?"

In short order, Cade selected a pair of high-topped Tony's—dark brown and cream tooled leather with pull holes. Fancier than he normally would've chosen, but the boots fit like a glove. Felt as if he'd been wearing them for a week.

"You'll want some saddle soap and polish for those," Maura said. "To make 'em last. At that price, you'd better."

"I'm not one to polish my boots all that much," he said.

Maura tsked. "Well, you need to. Keeping the leather clean will make 'em last longer, and polish looks nice—especially when you go dancing." She winked.

But instead of remembering the dance he'd shared with Maura at the barbecue, Cade thought of Reno.

He hadn't seen her since he'd kissed her, and he felt like a weasel for not going out to check on her. But she'd shaken him. She obviously didn't want to pursue anything with him. But it was hard to accept she was in love with Pritchard.

"How's Reno doing?" he heard himself asking as Maura handed him a can of saddle soap.

"Not bad. I've been helping her on my days off, and Wynonna's making sure she takes it easy, which is driving them both crazy."

"I'm sure."

"Why don't you stop by and see her?" Maura said. "I'm sure she'd be grateful for the visit."

Reno had enough visitors, Cade suspected. Maura was obviously aware of his attraction to Reno. Was he that easy to read?

"Maybe I will," he said noncommittally.

"Darn it, we're out of the shade of brown polish you need," she murmured, perusing the selection stacked on a shelf near the service counter. "Tell you what. The boot repair shop carries the same brand. They'd probably have it. Do you know where it is?"

"I do." Unless they'd moved. "Sixth and Main?" he asked.

"That's the one."

"Thanks, Maura."

"No problem. Anything else I can help you with?"

He hesitated. He'd be spending enough buying the boots, but he'd spotted a sale rack with pearl-snap Western shirts. Twenty-five percent off.

"I might grab a shirt or two," he said.

A short time later he left the store carrying a plastic bag, the boot box tucked under his arm. In the truck he switched his old cowboy boots for the new pair. Might as well start breaking them in.

The repair shop looked almost exactly as Cade remembered it. A few things had been rearranged, and a handful of folding chairs now lined one wall. A tall, tanned man sat in one, his black hair showing beneath his cowboy hat. Cade didn't recognize him, but it was easy to see the young man, probably in his mid to late twenties, was American Indian, with his high, angular cheekbones and thin upper lip. He studied Cade without being obvious.

Cade made his way toward the front counter, enjoying the sweet smell of leather permeating the air.

A heavyset man wearing a cowboy hat that had seen better days came out of the back room. "Cade Lantana, is that you?" A grin split his face. "Lord 'a mercy." He held out his hand, grasping Cade's while simultaneously cuffing him on the shoulder.

"It's me all right, Larry."

"I heard you were back—sorry I missed the barbecue. Hang on a minute, and I'll be right with you." He disappeared through the doorway to the rear room again. Cade could see a workbench from where he stood. Larry appeared to be putting the finishing touches on resoling a pair of black cowboy boots.

Belatedly, it registered that the guy waiting in the folding chair was in his stocking feet. Cade tried not to stare, but his curiosity grew. Unlike where he lived in Idaho, near a reservation outside of New Meadows, not that many Native Americans lived in Eagle's Nest. Of course, there were Reno and Wynonna....

"I've got your boots ready, buddy," Larry said, coming back out.

"Thank you," the man said, rising from the folding chair. He stood easily six-four. His black cowboy hat was pulled low on his forehead, and looked like it had seen quite a bit of trail dust. Was he a local? Had Larry called him "Buddy" or "buddy"?

The guy stepped into the boots, then took out his wallet to pay Larry. With a final nod toward Cade, he walked quietly from the store.

"Who was that?" Cade asked.

"Don't know." Larry shrugged. "Just some feller wanting his boots resoled and reheeled. Paid me extra to do it while he waited. Guess he didn't have a spare pair."

"Yeah, I know how that goes. I just picked up a new pair myself." Cade asked for the boot polish

Maura had recommended, and Larry plunked a two-inch-high glass jar in front of him.

"Got it. Anything else? Saddle soap?"

"Maura sold me some."

"All right then." Larry rang up the polish, and Cade was on his way.

Outside, he looked around, scanning the sidewalk for the dark-skinned cowboy. Across the street in front of the diner, near where Cade had left his own truck, a silver-blue Ford dually pickup with an extended cab and a black camper shell was parked. Thinking he could use a hamburger, Cade crossed the street. The Ford had Montana license plates. He heard a low growl from inside the truck, and through the open window he spotted the biggest Doberman pinscher he'd ever seen. The dog had to weigh a good hundred pounds.

"Take it easy, pal," Cade said.

Though the Dobie could've easily lunged out the truck window, it only lifted its lips at him.

Cade loved dogs, but Dobies scared him. He knew they likely didn't all deserve their bad reputation, but with its cropped ears and piercing eyes, this black-and-rust-colored animal looked more than a little intimidating.

Cade put his boot polish in his own truck, then pushed through the diner door. The guy with the black cowboy hat was sitting at the counter, perusing a menu. He flirted with the cute, dark-haired waitress as he ordered a club sandwich and fries. Cade chose a vacant stool two seats over.

"You following me?" the man said, his mouth lifting at the corners. His dark eyes sparkled.

Cade hooked his thumbs in his belt hoops. "Not if you're the owner of that badass dog sitting in the front seat of that Ford." He gestured over his shoulder toward the diner's picture window.

The man laughed quietly. "He doesn't bite. Unless he needs to."

Cade held out his hand. "Cade Lantana."

"Dakota Adair." He had a firm, strong grip, with no macho posturing.

"I see you're from Montana."

"Yep."

The waitress poured Cade a cup of black coffee as he waved away a menu.

"So, what brings you down our way?" Cade asked when she'd left.

Dakota swallowed a bite of club sandwich. "I'm on vacation."

"Visiting family?"

"Just passing through. Doing some fishing here and there."

"You paid for a nonresident license?"

Dakota raised an eyebrow. "You the game warden?"

"BLM," Cade replied, stretching the truth.

"I bought a three-day temporary."

"So, what do you do back in Montana?"

"I'm a saddle maker."

"Really?" Cade had always wanted a custom-made saddle, but the cost was more than he could justify. "Guess you can keep your own hours that way."

"Pretty much. So long as I fill my orders. Lets me hunt and fish when and where I want."

"Can't beat that," Cade said. He sipped his coffee. Wouldn't a saddle maker be able to resole his own cowboy boots? And wasn't there plenty of fishing in Montana—with even more trout than Colorado's western slope had to offer?

Then again, some sportsmen simply found pleasure in fishing and hunting in different states, and Cade supposed a saddle maker might get tired enough of his own trade to want someone else to fix his boots for him.

The two men chatted more before Dakota finished his sandwich. Leaving enough cash on the counter to cover his bill and a generous tip, he stood. "See you around."

Cade nodded. Maybe he was letting his imagination and suspicions work overtime. At any rate, once he'd finished his coffee, he crossed the street to the repair shop again.

"Back so soon?" Larry asked.

"I've got an odd question for you."

"Shoot." The graying man wiped his big hands on a tattered rag.

"That fella that was in here a little bit ago—you said he got his boots repaired?"

Larry nodded. "The soles were pretty worn, but he could've gotten more mileage out of them. The heels, too."

"What did you do with the old ones?"

"Threw 'em in the trash," Larry said. "Why?"

"Can I have them?"

His old friend gave him a strange look. "Thought your Tony Lamas were new. You hard up for spare parts?" He guffawed.

"Let's just say I'm running with a hunch."

"This have something to do with the poachers?" Larry wasn't the only one in town who knew Cade had been helping Sam. "You don't think that guy—"

"I don't think anything for sure yet," Cade stated.

"Got you. Well, since the soles and heels are in the trash, I guess that pretty much makes them my property," Larry told him. "Public property once I throw them in the Dumpster, which I would've tonight." He fished them out and put the pieces in a plastic bag. "Knock yourself out, cowboy."

RENO DIDN'T CARE one bit that Cade hadn't been in touch with her for over a week. She'd been hanging out with Austin.

Which was why she felt so irritated when the sight of Cade's truck and trailer pulling into her driveway made her stomach churn. Checking her hair in the mirror, she felt even more ridiculous. She'd put it in two braids today, with Wynonna's help. The cast wouldn't come off for another five weeks, and Reno was sure she'd lose her mind by then. She could hardly even move her fingers.

"Hair's fine," she mumbled, stalking out onto the front porch.

To further annoy her, the dogs greeted Cade like he was an old friend.

Well, wasn't he?

"What's up?" Reno leaned casually against the support beam at the top of the steps.

He looked even better than he had at the picnic—when he'd kissed her. He was dressed in what looked like a new shirt. Black, patterned with white bucking broncs, pearl snaps... He needed a haircut, but that only made him more attractive, reminding her of the wild bronc rider she'd once known.

"New boots?" Reno asked, eyeing his feet.

"Yeah, got 'em this morning." He pulled his pant leg up to show them off, then shook it back into place.

"What brings you here? Any news?"

"Not really. But I wanted to show you something." He started up the steps, and Reno noted he had a plastic bag in his hand.

"What the heck is that?" she asked, when he pulled something out.

"Boot sole. Two of them, as a matter of fact, with heels to match."

Reno drew back. "Have you been drinking?"

He gave a dry laugh. "No." He told her about the man he'd seen in town and talked to at the diner.

Reno's blood chilled. "You think he's one of the poachers?"

"Could be. He's from out of state, and these soles and heels aren't worn enough to warrant replacing. So what other reason could he have than to change the appearance of his footprints?"

"Sounds like he's smart," Reno said, impressed. *And so was Cade.* She took a sole and examined it. The worn number in the arch indicated size eleven. "Big guy."

Cade nodded. "Taller than me by a couple inches."

"Did he have a horse trailer?"

"No, but he could have it parked somewhere."

"And he was alone?"

"Other than the biggest damn dog I've ever seen, yeah." He told her about the Doberman, and Reno laughed.

"Why, Cade, I didn't think you were scared of anything."

"Not scared, just respectful."

"So, what's next?" She indicated his horse trailer. "You going to take Jet out?"

The Harlequin Reader Service — Here's how it works:

Accepting your 2 free books and 2 free mystery gifts places you under no obligation to buy anything. You may keep the books and gifts and return the shipping statement marked "cancel". If you do not cancel, about a month later we'll send you 6 additional books and bill you just $4.69 each in the U.S. or $5.24 each in Canada. That is a savings of at least 15% off the cover price. It's quite a bargain! Shipping and handling is just 25¢ per book, along with any applicable taxes.* You may cancel at any time, but if you choose to continue, every month we'll send you 6 more books, which you may either purchase at the discount price or return to us and cancel your subscription.

*Terms and prices subject to change without notice. Sales tax applicable in N.Y. Canadian residents will be charged applicable provincial taxes and GST. Offer not valid in Quebec. All orders subject to approval. Credit or debit balances in a customer's account(s) may be offset by any other outstanding balance owed by or to the customer. Please allow 4 to 6 weeks for delivery. Offer available while quantities last.

Do You Have the LUCKY KEY?

PLAY THE *Lucky Key Game*
and you can get

FREE BOOKS and FREE GIFTS!

Scratch the gold areas with a coin. Then check below to see the books and gifts you can get!

YES!
I have scratched off the gold areas. Please send me the 2 FREE BOOKS and 2 FREE GIFTS, worth about $10, for which I qualify. I understand I am under no obligation to purchase any books, as explained on the back of this card.

336 HDL EVKT   **135 HDL EVN5**

FIRST NAME	LAST NAME

ADDRESS

APT.#	CITY

STATE/PROV.	ZIP/POSTAL CODE

www.eHarlequin.com

2 free books plus 2 free gifts   1 free book

2 free books   Try Again!

Offer limited to one per household and not valid to current subscribers of Harlequin Superromance® books.
Your Privacy – Harlequin Books is committed to protecting your privacy. Our Privacy Policy is available online at www.eHarlequin.com or upon request from the Harlequin Reader Service. From time to time we make our lists of customers available to reputable third parties who may have a product or service of interest to you. If you would prefer for us not to share your name and address, please check here. ☐

He nodded. "I thought I might go up above the canyon where the poachers parked their rigs that night. It hasn't rained since then, so maybe some footprints will still be intact. So far, the casts Pritchard's deputies took haven't turned up anything, so maybe I can do a comparison with the boot soles. I'll look by your paddock, too, but I'd say those prints are long gone."

"More than likely." If this Dakota guy had harmed one hair of her horses' manes...well, she wanted him as badly as Cade did. More. "Mind if I ride with you?" she asked.

"Why?"

"Cade, I can't sit still, wondering who's responsible for taking the mustangs. I want to be there to see the prints myself."

"Suit yourself. But even if these old boot soles match up, it wouldn't really prove anything. You can't lock a man away just because he walked on a dirt road."

"Then I'll file trespassing charges," Reno said, ticked off that Cade was right. Her throbbing wrist wasn't doing much for her mood. She wanted someone to pay for stealing her mustangs, and if that someone was Dakota...well, she'd plant a boot in his ass, no matter how big he and his dog were.

"I guess you could," Cade said. "But wouldn't you rather wait and catch him trying to take more horses? That way we can lock him up for a long while. Trespassing, you'll be lucky to get him a slap on the wrist."

"True."

"Sam's been camping in the area," Cade said. "Maybe he ought to back off. Let the poachers think he's looking somewhere else."

"That's a gamble. They could roll in here and take more horses if Sam's not watching."

"Oh, we'll be watching all right," Cade said. "They just won't know it."

CHAPTER TEN

AFTER TALKING TO CADE yesterday, Reno was more determined than ever to remain vigilant. She and Cade had ridden out to check out his boot track theory, and sure enough, Dakota Adair's footprints were in the damp soil near the watering hole, though Cade hadn't found any in the area where the poachers had parked their rigs. Still, what had he been doing at the former site? Reno had phoned Austin, and he'd promised to check the guy out.

Sitting at her computer now, Reno pecked at the keyboard with one hand, finding it difficult to focus as she worked on the monthly budget for the ranch and the sanctuary. They'd gotten several generous donations for the mustangs recently, likely a result of the publicity the poachers had caused. She supposed at least some small amount of good had come from all the bad.

Reno was thinking about shutting down the computer as the phone rang, and she was filled with a sense of déjà vu. *Cade?* But it was Austin. "You getting cabin fever yet?" he asked.

She grunted. "And how. It's driving me crazy, not being able to do chores. I don't know what I'd do without my friends helping me out."

"You want to go get a bite to eat?"

Reno glanced at the clock. Lunchtime had sneaked up on her. "I'd love to."

"Or if you're up to it, we could skip lunch in town. A horseback ride and a picnic sounds—"

Like something she'd done with Cade.

"You know, I've had a hankering for a cheeseburger and fries all morning."

"Okay," Austin said. "I'll pick you up in a few."

Reno finished up her work on the computer, then shut it down.

A half hour later, she was riding shotgun in Austin's patrol car, with an actual shotgun propped against the middle of the seat to the left of her knee, stock resting on the floorboard. The police radio hummed in the background, the dispatcher's voice calling out codes Reno always found fascinating, wondering what they meant. She liked riding in Austin's cruiser, seeing his job firsthand. She found the whole business of looking out for lawbreakers and bringing them to justice exciting. Maybe she should go to the police academy, take up a career in law enforcement.

Naw. With her temper, she'd probably shoot

some fool who deserved it, and end up on the wrong side of the bars.

"You're enjoying this, aren't you?" Austin grinned.

"Always. I couldn't do your job, though."

"Why's that?"

"My ancestors settled things the old-fashioned way—an eye for an eye. Grandpa Mel believed in the same retribution."

Austin grunted. "Tell me you're not going to string up those poachers if—make that when—we get ahold of them."

"Somebody will have to hold me back. So, did you talk to Dakota Adair?"

"Not yet. I'm not sure where he's camping. Unfortunately, the matching tracks don't mean anything."

Reno didn't bother to hide her disappointment. "Why not?"

"Cade was right, Reno. About all I could get the guy for is trespassing."

Reno collapsed against the headrest. "I'm getting pretty frustrated."

"Join the club." Austin pulled up in front of the diner. "Speaking of ol' sharp eyes…"

Cade's Chevy was parked out front.

Reno wondered if the two men would get into another macho preening match. If the expression on Cade's face as she entered with Austin was any indication, she was right on the mark.

"What are you doing, playing cop?" he asked Reno as she and Austin slid into a booth opposite his. Cade smelled like a million bucks, looked even better. "Or robbers?" He glared at the sheriff, and Reno fought to clamp her jaw shut.

Was Cade insinuating Austin was robbing him of his girl? Ridiculous, since she sure wasn't that. Cade was definitely jealous. A little thrill fluttered in her chest, and Reno tamped it down. Now she *was* being ridiculous.

It had been only a few kisses.

On a picnic blanket…at their favorite spot.

She wished the two men would just put their heads together and catch the damn poachers.

"What're you up to, Cade?" Austin asked. "Find any more old boots to investigate?" He laughed.

Cade's eyes narrowed. "The prints matched."

"That they did, but I'm not sure what to do with the information."

"Maybe start by questioning Dakota Adair?" Cade suggested dryly.

"Well, now that might be an idea, except that I've no idea where to find the guy. He comes in the diner now and then, I hear, so I figure that's my best bet to run into him."

"And you needed to bring Reno with you for…?"

"Why, for the pleasure of her company," Austin drawled, purposely raking his gaze over her.

Lucky for them, she had a cast on. Or she'd wring their necks. Maybe she ought to bop them over their heads with it.

Letting Reno order first, Austin told the waitress what he wanted, then excused himself to go to the men's room.

Cade immediately slipped into the sheriff's vacated seat. "What are you doing, Reno? I mean, really? That guy's a waste of your time. He's too full of himself. Thinks he's God's gift to women."

"Is that right?" She leaned on her good elbow, resting her chin on her fist and giving him a faux smile. "I'll go out with whomever I please."

Before he could answer, the sheriff was back. "Want to join us, Cade? No sense in taking up two booths."

"I was leaving anyway," he said. He rose, threw some bills onto his table and strode out of the diner.

"Now what in the world do you suppose is wrong with him?" Austin asked. He grinned. "Guess he's jealous I'm having lunch with the prettiest woman in the county."

"Don't let Wynonna hear you say that," Reno said, trying to lighten the mood. Trying not to think about Cade. "She'll be the jealous one."

Austin chuckled. "I think Barry Biltmore's already got his eye on her."

Their lunch arrived, and Reno relished the tasty burger and enjoyable company. She liked Austin.

Still, he wasn't Cade.

"Say," Reno said, when they'd finished eating, "do you think you can drop me off at the cemetery?"

"The cemetery?" Austin pulled out his wallet to pay the bill. "That's a heck of a way to end a lunch date."

"I want to visit Mom's and Grandpa and Grandma's graves." Trying not to think about Cade and the past made her realize she hadn't been to the cemetery in too long. "I'll call Wynonna on my cell phone when I'm ready to go home. She'll be in town for her crafts club meeting, anyway."

"Well, if that's what you want." He shrugged.

Minutes later, he dropped her off at Eagle's Nest Memorial Gardens. "Thanks, Austin," she said.

"Thank you." He moved to give her a kiss, but Reno pulled back.

"Not while you're on duty," she cautioned. "We can't have folks in town seeing the sheriff kissing women in his squad car."

"I'm not kissing any other women," Austin said, eyes twinkling. "But I'll take a rain check."

"See you later." Reno closed the door and breathed a sigh of relief when he drove away. What was wrong with her? She'd kissed Austin dozens of times.

She walked through the cemetery, with its view of the mountains and scattered cottonwood trees shading the rows of headstones. Grandpa Mel was buried near Grandma Belle beneath one of those trees, his tombstone black marble. His name and the dates were all he'd requested, but Reno had gone a step further.

She'd had a photo of Mel in his thirties, on his favorite horse—a bay-and-white paint—embossed into the stone. In the photo, her grandfather wore his hair long beneath a cowboy hat. He looked young and strong, and most of all, happy. Her grandmother had died of breast cancer a year later. Mel had been alone until Wynonna, and then Reno's mother, came from Montana to live with him on the ranch.

Reno sat cross-legged in the grass in front of the marker. "How're you doing, Grandfather? Grandmother?" She spoke a few words in Apache. Then she said a prayer and got to her feet. "I promise you, Grandfather, I'll find those poachers, and I'll get Storm-Bringer back. Somehow, I will." Reno's eyes burned.

She only hoped it wasn't too late for the mare with the lightning bolt marking. The mare she believed carried a piece of her grandfather's spirit.

Taking a deep breath, she walked across the neatly clipped lawn. One row over from Grandpa Mel, her mother was buried. Reno had bought the closest available plot to her mom and grandma when her grandfather died. She wished Carlina or

Grandpa Mel would've planned ahead and bought a family plot, but neither had. How many people made the same mistake, not thinking anything would happen…until it was too late?

Carlina had been just thirty-six when she died, Grandpa Mel gone only months after his sixtieth birthday.

"Mom." Reno sank to the ground. She needed to bring flowers next time. She fingered the heart locket on the chain she'd draped over her mother's headstone. In a bigger town, it might've been stolen. In Eagle's Nest, people had more respect than that.

As she held the locket, Reno gave in to tears. Quietly, she sobbed, "I miss you so much, Mom. Why did you have to leave me?"

It hit her then that, deep down, she blamed her mother. How could she have turned a blind eye to Sonny's sickness? Surely, Carlina had seen. How could she not have?

Their family had been torn apart when Sonny raped and killed a girl Reno went to school with. Then the police had gathered evidence from Sonny's computer, showing the pedophilia he'd kept secret. He'd even molested an eleven-year-old girl years earlier, before he met Carlina, and had pleaded a reduced sentence. The police also turned up records from a town fifty miles away. It turned out Sonny had raped a fifteen-year-old when Reno was a small child. The girl and her mother were too afraid of him to testify, and the charges had been dropped.

If Carlina had known her husband's true nature, she'd chosen to turn a blind eye. Reno squeezed the locket so tightly, she felt the imprint of the gold etching bite into her palm. Surely Carlina hadn't seen any signs. How *could* she have ignored them?

Reno relaxed her fist and let the locket fall back against the headstone. Sonny had been arrested and put in jail to await trial, but he'd somehow managed to come up with the bail the judge had set at his arraignment. Reno shook her head, staring at her mother's name. How had he gotten the money? Surely not from her mom…. Was that why Carlina had killed herself? She'd never know. Sonny had hidden in an abandoned house outside of town, where Cade and the other lawmen tracked him down. Sonny had already decided he'd rather die than go to prison, and die he did. Suicide by cop… He'd pointed a semiautomatic pistol directly at Cade, who'd had to respond.

Reno sat back on her heels and dried her tears. "Mom, why? I needed you more than you needed…" Pills. Tranquilizers, booze. Anything Carlina could get her hands on. Including that final, lethal cocktail of all three.

Standing, Reno wiped the dirt and grass off her

jeans. What would she have done without Wynonna? Reno glanced at her watch, then dialed Wy's cell number.

CADE COULDN'T GET the bitter taste out of his mouth, the one that had ruined his lunch as soon as he'd seen Reno with Pritchard. It was none of his business. What did he expect her to do—break up with Pritchard, abandon her ranch and move to Idaho with him one day?

Hardly.

A few minutes later his cell phone rang, and Wynonna asked a favor of him. One he couldn't bring himself to refuse.

"Reno's at the cemetery," she said. "She called and asked me for a ride home, but I can't get away right now. Can you pick her up?"

So instead of heading for the BLM office to see Sam, he drove toward Eagle's Nest Memorial Gardens. He wondered how often Reno visited Mel's grave and her mother's and grandma's. She must miss them something fierce.

Cade hated to think of the illness that was bound to claim his dad sooner or later. He tried not to; no one knew when his or her time was up for sure. Anything could happen. Cade himself could be in an accident, or suddenly find out he had some deadly disease. Things like that occurred to people every day.

Maybe his father would live longer than anyone expected. Cade prayed so. Still, one way or another, he would have to return to Idaho at some point.

He swung into the small cemetery and drove slowly past the rows of headstones until he spotted Reno standing beneath a towering cottonwood. The sadness on her face gave way to surprise as he opened the door and got out.

"Wynonna asked me to give you a lift home," he said, as he walked over to her.

She looked beautiful, standing there beneath the tree, her faded jeans molded to her slender yet curvy figure. She had long legs, and her black hair fell down her back in a ponytail beneath her cowboy hat. He remembered how it had looked at the barbecue, long, loose, silky.

"Why?" she asked, jarring him from his musings.

"Why what? Oh—she couldn't leave her crafts club thing or something like that." He shrugged. "Want a ride?"

Seeing Reno's expression, Cade almost laughed out loud. Wy had set this up, and he hadn't suspected a thing.

He couldn't help but grin. No matter what his better judgment told him, he was always happy to find an excuse to spend time with Reno. *Thank you, Wynonna.*

"Okay," Reno said. "Thanks." She stepped forward, holding her cast slightly away from her body.

"Your wrist bothering you much?"

"More than I'd thought it would."

He opened the passenger-side door for her, and she glared at him. "I still have one good arm."

"Get in. Stubborn woman."

"Pushy man."

She climbed into the Chevy, and he reached across to buckle her seat belt for her, enjoying the way she squirmed. She smelled like heaven. Berries, daisies…something sweet and wild. It was all he could do to draw back once the shoulder belt was in place. Cade closed the door, then walked around the front end to the driver's side.

Reno didn't have much to say to him as he tried to make small talk all the way to Wild Horse Ranch. When he parked near the house, she reached to unbuckle her seat belt before he could help her.

As the catch slid loose, he laid his hand over hers. "Reno." He looked her in the eye. "Do you really resent me that much?"

"What're you talking about?"

"You know. Are you truly that mad at me for moving to Idaho? I mean, it was so long ago…."

She gave a dry laugh. "*So long ago?* You're kidding me, right?"

"Well, it was."

"So, because it's been nine years, I'm supposed

to have no feelings about what happened?" Reno clenched her teeth. If he didn't know better, he'd think she was about to cry.

"But I was hurting, too," Cade said. "I had to do something to keep from going crazy. I had to leave."

"So, that's it? You just did what was best for you, and to heck with anyone else?"

"No." He pulled back, her words cutting him like a razor. "Reno, I cared about you. More than you can know." He'd loved her. Wrong, given her age, but there it was. He had loved Reno…and still did.

"Yeah, that's why you left when my mom died."

Cade took a deep breath. Heaven knew, he hadn't intended to hurt her.

"You haven't really forgiven me. Reno, I wish you would."

Tears began to fall down her cheeks, and Reno wiped them away angrily. She was still angry. "I've tried," she said. "I'll try harder. Not that I really have to, given that you'll be leaving again eventually." As soon as the words were out, she looked contrite. "Cade, I'm sorry. I wish your dad many more years. Really, I do. I'm sorry for what your family is going through."

"I appreciate that."

She lifted her chin. "I know I need to put the past away, Cade, for me. I'm just not sure how to go about doing it."

"I wish I had an answer. Reno, I know you always thought of me as a big brother—"

"For a while I did," she interrupted.

Hellfire. He was trying to explain to her that he'd never thought of himself as her big brother. Quite the opposite. The words scrambled in his brain and didn't come out the way he wanted. "But, Reno…that's not how I felt."

She shut up. That quick, she was speechless, which in turn left him struggling for the next words.

"I guess I figured that out by the way you kissed me the other day," she finally said, letting him off the hook. "But nothing's changed, Cade. You're still planning to go back to Idaho, and I still refuse to let you hurt me again."

He set his jaw. He'd wanted to kiss her again. "I don't want to hurt you, either," he said.

Reno opened her door and got out.

"Call me if you need anything," Cade told her. "I mean it."

She hesitated, leaning on the open door. "I do appreciate everything you're doing for me—for the mustangs."

He forced a smile. "You had it right the first time."

She closed the door and walked away.

What the hell was he going to do?

Driving away from Wild Horse Ranch, Cade searched for answers he was sure he'd never find.

CHAPTER ELEVEN

RENO DROVE TO THE CO-OP on Friday. She preferred
the down-home customer service and the smaller,
more intimate atmosphere. Not to mention the
prices were usually lower than Ted's. That it was
two miles closer to Wild Horse Ranch didn't hurt,
either, since she found it awkward to drive with her
cast on. She had to shift and steer with her right
hand, using the cast to hold the wheel whenever she
changed gears.

Wynonna had offered to run her errands for her,
but Reno needed to get out, alone. She still had
muddled feelings for Cade. It was two days since
she'd seen him, and already she missed him. What
in the world would she do once he moved back to
Idaho?

Inside the co-op, Reno waited her turn behind
a couple of ranchers she knew. They made small
talk, asking after her broken wrist, wanting details
of how the injury had happened. She was retell-
ing the way-too-familiar story when, out of the

corner of her eye, she saw someone watching her—a middle-aged man in a gray cowboy hat who looked vaguely familiar. He requested several hundred pounds of sweet feed, and as he waited for the salesperson to write up his receipt, he smiled at Reno.

"I don't mean to interrupt, but aren't you Reno Blackwell?" When she nodded, he held out his hand. "I'm Chet McPherson, Maura's dad."

"Of course." She'd seen him in town before. "Nice to meet you." Reno shook his hand. "Your daughter has been a lifesaver, Mr. McPherson." She held her cast aloft. "I'll be *so* glad to get this thing off."

He quirked his mouth. "So Maura says. And call me Chet. You know, you're doing her mother and me a favor, too, letting Maura volunteer at your sanctuary. She's not cut out to be a sheep rancher."

"I can tell how much she loves horses. Reminds me of myself a few years ago, actually. Guess I haven't changed much." With her right index finger, she tried to scratch an unreachable itch beneath the cast.

"Well, I just wanted you to know you're certainly not imposing on her."

"Thanks, I appreciate it."

Chet tipped his hat. "See you around, Reno."

"Sure." Reno waved, then gave her order for grain to Rick at the counter. A short time later, her Chevy loaded with eight fifty-pound bags of sweet feed—which she had no hope of moving to the barn—Reno drove homeward. She dialed Shelly on her cell, got her voice mail, then tried Maura.

"Hey, Reno."

"Hey. Guess who I just met at the co-op? Your dad."

"The traitor!" Maura said. "What was Dad doing buying feed there instead of at Ted's?"

"I don't know, but he sure is nice. He told me how much you love coming out to the ranch."

"You know I do."

"Good. Because I've got a whole bunch of grain that needs unloading, and I hate to ask Wynonna. She can do it, but…"

"Say no more. I'm off work in ten minutes."

"So, you don't consider *me* a traitor?"

"No." She laughed. "I'll meet you at your place."

"Thanks, Maura." Reno closed her phone and laid it on the seat.

Behind her, red and blue lights flashed, and she looked in her rearview mirror to see Austin's squad car. *What now?* Maybe he had news about the poachers. Reno pulled onto the shoulder and shut off her truck.

"Hey, Austin," she said as he walked up to her open window.

He looked solemn. "Reno, what are you doing?"

"What do you mean?" Had she been driving too fast?

"You've got a cast on your left arm, which basically renders it useless, and yet you're driving a standard, and using a cell phone while you steer…with what? Your knees?"

He was right. She should've pulled over to call Maura.

"I'm sorry." She gave him a wide-eyed, innocent look. "I guess I wasn't thinking."

He rested his forearm on the top of her door, leaning closer. "I ought to write you a ticket," he said. Then he smiled. "But I suppose I can let you off with a warning. Of course, that means you owe me one."

"Sure. Name it."

"How about dinner tomorrow night? I'll take you to the steak house."

His offer didn't hold the appeal it once would have. But what could she say? "That sounds good."

"Great." His smile widened. "Pick you up at six-thirty?"

"Sure."

He pulled out a pen.

"Hey, I thought you weren't writing me up."

"Hold out your arm."

Ah. Reno stuck her cast through the window. Austin scratched the pen across it for a minute, then winked. "Catch you later."

He waited for her to pull away first. With a wave, Reno started the Chevy and, careful to check her mirrors, pulled back onto the road. She didn't look at the cast until she was nearly to the house. Next to Cade's signature and well wishes, Austin had written, "Reno, take it easy. Looking forward to Saturday night."

Crud! She knew Austin had purposely put his note and signature where Cade was bound to notice….

She wanted to scribble over the words—cross them out with black marker. But that would only draw more attention to them.

At the ranch, Wynonna came outside and offered to unload the grain, of course. Reno gave her a hug. "Thanks, but Maura's on her way over to do it."

"Are you insinuating I'm too old and fat to lift a feed bag?"

"Hardly. Truth is, I'd hate to have you show me up. Maura's a couple years younger than me, so that's a whole different story."

Wynonna gave her a playful shove. "You're full of it, girl." Then she looked over Reno's shoulder. "Who in the world is that?"

Reno followed her gaze. In the distance, coming through the sagebrush, she saw a rider on a liver chestnut horse—an uncommon color. The guy wore a black cowboy hat and a light shirt.

"I don't know, but he's trespassing." She supposed it could be a neighbor. But Reno didn't recognize the horse, and the rider was too far away to make out his features.

He rode toward them, slowly, hesitantly, then pulled the horse up short. The chestnut bobbed its head.

"Hello!" Reno called, waving.

"Reno, be careful." Wynonna laid a hand on her arm. "Who would be riding across the sagebrush like that?"

Who indeed?

The cowboy abruptly turned the horse around and set off at a lope, then a gallop.

Reno tossed her cell phone at Wynonna. "Call Austin—no, Cade," she said, racing for the barn. *Hell.* The guy had to be up to no good.

Behind her, she heard Wynonna saying something, but couldn't make it out. Reno rushed to Plenty Coups's stall. She didn't want to alarm the sheriff's office for no reason. But why did the guy on the horse run? She was damned if she'd let him get away.

One-handed, she fumbled with the latch on the stall, then grabbed Plenty Coups's halter.

"Let me help you," Wynonna said from behind her. "Cade's on his way."

The blue roan ducked his head, and Reno slid the halter on him.

"Maybe you should wait," Wy suggested.

"I can't. This is the closest we've come to one of the poachers. If he's not…well, what is he doing on my land? And why run?"

"Should I call Austin, too?"

Reno dropped a saddle blanket onto Plenty Coups's back. "I don't know. Maybe." Her head swam.

"Let me help you," Wynonna said again, taking the lightweight barrel racing saddle Reno had pulled from the tack room, and lifting it onto the horse.

Reno had Plenty Coups through the barn door moments later, and was galloping across the range after the stranger by the time Cade pulled up in her driveway.

RENO SLOWED Plenty Coups to a walk, scanning the ground. She'd followed the set of shod hoofprints until they disappeared among the rocks.

"He's got to be somewhere," she mumbled. She sent Plenty Coups up the side of the mountain, looking for any sign of the rider's passage.

Thirty minutes later, she'd run out of clues. She'd spotted old tracks—some shod, some not— and a few places where the brush looked trampled. But whether it was from the lone cowboy coming through or from her own horses, who knew? Reno didn't see any dirt or grass freshly turned up by galloping hooves.

At the sound of hoofbeats, her heart began to pound. Reno looked up to see Cade riding toward her on Honey.

"There you are," he said, scowling. "What were you thinking, taking off like that, Reno?"

"I lost him." Reno slapped her pommel in frustration. "Did Wynonna call Austin?"

"I told her not to. I didn't see any point in Pritchard racing out here until we found out who the guy on the horse was. Are you sure he wasn't a neighbor?"

"Positive." She described the rider as best she could. "He was on a liver chestnut with a flaxen mane and tail. I'd remember a horse like that! Plus my neighbors would ride up the driveway, not cut across the back of my property."

"Okay." Cade scanned the ground. "So, you're not sure which of these tracks are his?"

"I lost his trail on the rocks below and picked up these prints here." She pointed. "Could belong to another rider or even my horses when they were taken." Reno clenched her fist. "Damn it, I was so close! It'll take us hours…days, maybe…to figure out which tracks are his. By then, the guy'll be gone."

"I'm not giving up," Cade said. "This is the closest I've been to finding somebody who might have some answers."

"I'm game to keep riding if you are."

He shook his head. "Go back to the house, Reno. Wynonna's worried sick, and there's nothing you can do that I can't do by myself." She started to protest, but he cut her off. "Hey, I'm sorry if I was hard on you at the cemetery, and that I acted like a jerk at the diner."

"It doesn't matter."

"Well, I'm still sorry. If you want to go out with Austin…that's your business." He hesitated. "Your arm's bothering you, isn't it?"

She shrugged. "Maybe a little."

"Go back to the house," he repeated. "I'll be there as soon as I can." Before she could argue, Cade swung Honey around and loped away.

IT WAS NEARLY DARK by the time Cade returned. Reno had fallen asleep on the couch, only because Wynonna had forced her to take a pain pill, prop her arm up and get some rest. Even though Wy seldom handled the horses, she'd managed to unsaddle Plenty Coups and help Reno brush him down, before locking the gelding in the barn.

"Did you find the rider?" Wynonna asked Cade. The two of them stood in the doorway of the living room, while Reno willed her foggy mind to clear.

"No, but from Reno's description, I wonder if it might've been that fellow from the boot repair shop— Dakota. You said he seemed to be a pretty big guy, Reno, and that he was wearing a black cowboy hat."

"A lot of cowboys wear black hats," she replied, pointedly looking at his. Her own hat was black, as well.

"Who the heck do you think this Dakota is, anyway?" Wynonna asked.

"Not some guy just passing through fishing, if that was him. His three-day license was up a week ago."

"I know you're perfectly capable," Reno said, "but maybe we should call Austin."

"I already phoned Sam. He and Paul are going to be on the lookout."

"But you're not here in an official capacity," Reno argued, "and you said Sam's stretched thin. Besides, it can't hurt."

"You're right," Cade agreed. "Somebody definitely needs to find Dakota and question him. Why would he have taken off?"

"I'm sorry, I can barely keep my eyes open," Wynonna said, yawning. She pushed away from the doorway, excusing herself. "Make sure you stay put on that couch until you go to bed." She pointed at Reno. "Arm resting."

"I'll make her behave," Cade said.

"Good luck." But Wynonna squeezed Reno's shoulder affectionately. "Everything will work out, dear one. Try to get some sleep tonight."

Reno patted her hand. "See you in the morning."

"I left a fresh batch of cookies on the kitchen table," Wy said, "if you want a snack. 'Night, Cade."

"'Night, Wynonna."

Once they were alone, he came over and crouched beside Reno.

"What are you doing?" she asked.

"Making sure you follow orders."

Before she could protest, he'd taken her stocking feet and swung them from the floor to the couch, tugging her legs straight out in front of her.

"Hey. I already took a nap."

"Hush." He fluffed the pillow behind her back, plus the one beneath her wrist. Then he spread the afghan over her lap.

"It's too hot for that." Reno swallowed. Her temperature had risen, all right. She reached to remove the blanket, and saw Cade's eyes on her cast.

Gently, he took hold of her arm to read the writing on it. "Saturday night? You and Pritchard are still cozy, huh?"

Reno pulled out of his grasp. "What if we are?"

"Then I might have to kick his butt."

"Why? He's not the one going back to Idaho."

Damn. She didn't want Cade to know she thought day and night about him leaving.

He said nothing. Simply looked at her. And then he leaned down and kissed her.

Reno moaned, wrapping her good arm around his neck.

Before she knew it, he was stretched out on the couch beside her, careful of her injury. He nuzzled her neck and whispered, "Reno, I want to make love to you."

No matter what her head told her, she wanted him, too. In the worst way.

"Wynonna's here."

"I know." He brushed kisses against her neck. "Let's go someplace else."

"Stop," she said weakly, giving him a half-hearted push. "We're being stupid."

"Complete idiots," he agreed, then kissed her again.

He undid the first three snaps on her shirt, sliding his hand inside to caress her breasts. "Aww, man," he groaned, sneaking a peek at her red-and-black lace bra in the dim lamplight, "who would've guessed you're a Victoria's Secret kind of gal?"

Reno felt herself blush from her face down to her toes. She might wear boots, jeans and men's Western shirts, but she treated herself to the most lacy, feminine lingerie she could buy. It was her one feminine indulgence.

And beneath her jeans, she wore a matching thong. She pushed Cade's hands away before he could make that discovery, so he found his way back to her breasts. Burying his face against her, he kissed her there, teasing her nipples through the lace before moving back to her mouth. He dipped his tongue inside, tangling it with hers, then sprinkled kisses along her jaw, her earlobe, making her crazy.

Dear God, she wanted him. But more than that,

she wanted to love him. The thought scared her spitless. "Cade, stop." She pushed him again, and he gazed at her, perplexed.

"What's wrong, Reno?"

"I'm not looking for a quick roll in the hay," she said, sitting up. "Or in this case, on the couch."

"Neither am I."

"Okay, I'm sorry." Reno fastened the snaps on her shirt. "I know you're better than that. But this won't work, Cade."

"We can make it work. Reno, give me a chance."

"No." She bit back tears. "I'm not going to be abandoned again. My life is here. On this ranch... with my mustangs."

"Your mustangs. I might've known."

"Known what?" she asked, her voice rising in anger.

"That you'd hide behind your horses. Just like your grandfather."

"You leave Grandpa Mel out of this," Reno said, temper flaring. "He was a decent and honorable man. He took care of me when you left, and he gave me this ranch when he died. It was all he had, besides me, and I'm not going to give it up."

Cade stood. "I'm going to leave now, before I say something I'll regret." He tugged his hat into place. "Good night, Reno."

"Cade. Don't do this. Don't leave like this." She reached out to touch his arm, but he jerked away.

"Why not? It's what you expect of me, right?" He turned and made for the door.

Reno slumped on the couch, not sure if she wanted to go after him, or thank her lucky stars he had gone.

Before he could make her fall harder for him than she already had.

CHAPTER TWELVE

CADE SPENT Saturday morning trying to catch up on chores. He'd been replacing shingles on the roof of the barn yesterday when Wynonna had called, frantic, to tell him Reno had taken off after the mystery rider he believed was Dakota Adair.

Now Cade used hard work to take his mind off Reno's rejection. Her words had hit home last night, and even though he knew she was right, he'd lashed out at her because she'd hurt him. He didn't like the way she'd made him feel. As if he was using her.

Done with the roof earlier that morning, Cade had ridden Jet out to check the fence line on the upper pasture and make sure the cows were settling in. He let his mind wander, trying to imagine where he would park if he wanted to stay out of sight. He'd already checked the KOA campground a few miles from town and found no sign of Dakota Adair and his silver-blue Ford. Had he moved on?

Cade had also checked the only two motels in

town. He'd even asked around the diner, but while several people remembered seeing the young cowboy more than once, no one knew where he was or where he'd been staying.

There were countless places the guy could camp. Permits weren't required for BLM land, only for state parks. Finding Dakota Adair would be like looking for the proverbial needle in a haystack.

Disgusted, Cade rode back toward the ranch house. He had barely arrived in the stable yard when his mom came rushing out of the house toward him. The look on her chalk-white face scared the daylights out of him.

He leaped from the saddle. "Mom, what is it?"

"Your father…" She swallowed a sob as Cade reached for her.

"What?" Collapsed? Died? Had to go in the ambulance…?

"He took off on his horse."

"What?"

Estelle squeezed her eyes shut against her tears. "And he didn't take his oxygen."

Cade bit back a curse. "It's okay, Mom, I'll find him. When did he leave?"

"I'm not sure—about a half hour ago? I was on the phone with Wynonna, and when I hung up, he was gone. I looked everywhere and then I saw Juker was g-gone, too."

Cade gave her a hug. "Breathe, Mom. It'll be all

right. Call the sheriff's office and have them get an ambulance out here."

"I already did, and I called Wynonna back so Reno would know."

Cade vaulted into the saddle once more, his hands shaking so badly he could barely gather the reins. "I'll find him," he repeated.

"Hurry!"

It didn't take long to spot Juker's tracks. The fifteen-year-old quarter horse had hooves the size of dinner plates, and wore bigger shoes than any other animal on the place, except for his dad's packhorse. The prints led away from the barn on a worn dirt trail, then broke away where Matt had cut across the grass.

Headed for the hills.

Off the Diamond L.

MATTHEW SLID FROM THE saddle and sat on a large rock, holding Juker's reins in one hand. Looking out at the valley below him, he felt alive for the first time in months. Colorado had changed so much since his boyhood. Most of the wildlife had disappeared as more and more ranches and open land were turned into shopping malls and subdivisions. But here near Eagle's Nest there were still plenty of ranches, and thousands of acres of BLM land. A man could get lost if he wanted to, and that was exactly what Matt intended.

It would be months before they found what the buzzards hadn't picked from his bones in the high country. He'd rather go out of this world the same way he'd come in—kicking and screaming—than die in some damn hospital bed with a bunch of tubes and beeping machines hooked to his body.

And without his oxygen tank, he knew it was only a matter of time before he'd be unable to breathe at all.

Juker lowered his head and gave him a nudge. "What's the matter, fella, huh?" Matthew rubbed the flea-bitten gray's forehead. He'd owned the gelding since Juker was a two-year-old colt. "You're still in your prime, buddy. Not like me. 'Course, I guess fifty-nine's kind of like fifteen in horse years, huh? That is, it would be if I'd taken better care of myself."

He took the single cigarette from his shirt pocket and stuck it in his mouth. "But what's the use of living life if you can't enjoy it? When we get up high in that black timber, I'm going to take your saddle and bridle off you, ol' hoss. If you feel like running back to the ranch, well, that's fine. And if you don't, that's fine, too. Maybe you can hook up with those mustangs of Reno's. Cade's gonna have them poachers corralled any day now. I know he will."

Matt reached into his pocket and took out a lighter. The smooth, familiar surface felt comfortable in his hand as he flicked it open and lit the cigarette. Inhaling deeply, he let the smoke linger in his lungs before exhaling. Immediately, Matt felt light-headed, and a coughing fit gripped him. He fought for air, cussing in between hacking. For a minute, he thought he might pass out.

"Damn it," he said to Juker when he could finally breathe again. "What is it about these things that are so all-fired hard to give up?" He eyed the lit cigarette between his fingers, watching the smoke twist from the burning end like a ghostly snake. He'd stopped coughing but his breathing became labored after the second puff. By the third, he could scarcely draw air into his lungs. He began to regret not bringing the portable oxygen tank along.

Stubbing the cigarette out against the rock, Matt staggered to his feet. "Guess the black timber's out of the question, old boy." He coughed some more as he reached to undo Juker's cinch. "Guess this spot will have to do." He slid the saddle and blanket from the gelding's back, and the effort took every last bit of his energy.

He was reaching to unbuckle the throatlatch on Juker's bridle when the ground began to spin beneath him.

"Aw, hell."

Matthew fell at the horse's big feet, eyes closed, fighting to stay conscious. He'd thought dying—letting go—would be easy. Beside him, Juker lowered his head and began to graze. Seconds later, the freckled gray lifted his head and let out a whinny. Through a haze, Matt spotted a rider heading his way. A guy in a black cowboy hat, with a mean-looking dog loping alongside.

Maybe the dog would finish him off. Or maybe the man would run him over with the liver-colored horse.

He'd lost his hat when he'd keeled over, and the dog, a Doberman pinscher, stopped to sniff it, before lowering his head to investigate Matt's face. "Good boy," he mumbled. His vision blurred.

"Mister, can you hear me?" The young man's voice seemed to come through a fog as he knelt and patted Matt's cheeks. Maybe he was hallucinating.

He couldn't breathe.

"Help… Help me," he whispered.

"Matthew Lantana's missing," Wynonna said to Reno as soon as she found her, coming in from the yard. "He took off on his horse while Estelle and I were talking."

"Oh, no," Reno said. "Where to?"

Wynonna shrugged. "She's not sure. Cade went to look for him, and Estelle called the sheriff's dispatch for an ambulance to be on hand. Matt doesn't have oxygen with him."

"The crazy fool," Reno said, already striding for the door. She put her hat back on and grabbed the keys to her truck. "Phone Estelle and tell her I'm on my way with Maura."

"Be careful," Wynonna called as Reno rushed outside.

Maura was in the arena, exercising one of the horses, when Reno reached her. "Cade needs our help," she cried.

"What's the matter?"

Quickly, Reno filled her friend in. "I don't normally haul horses with their tack on—" she indicated the palomino Maura was riding "—but just load him in the trailer as soon as we get it hooked up. I'll get Plenty Coups." Austin would likely form a search party to look for Matt, and she wanted to be part of it.

"Wait," Maura cautioned, quickly dismounting. "I'll get him. You hurt yourself worse, you won't be able to help anyone."

"Okay, but hurry."

With practiced ease, Reno backed her truck up to her two-horse trailer. Within minutes, she and Maura had the horses loaded, and were on their way. Pulse racing, Reno drove as fast as she dared, towing the trailer. It felt like forever before she reached the Diamond L. Austin and two deputies—J. T. Carver and Trent Jackson—were already there.

Austin was on horseback. "Reno, how'd you get here so fast?"

"Estelle called. Any word on Matt?"

"We're going to look for him. J.T. and Trent will organize a search party, but I'm heading out now. I don't think we've got any time to waste."

"Neither do I." Not with Matt having no oxygen. Reno faced Estelle, who'd rushed outside from the house, while Maura saddled Plenty Coups. "Which way did he ride?"

"I don't know where Matt went for sure, but Cade took off that way." She pointed toward the distant hills to the west.

"Okay. Try to stay calm, Estelle. We're going to find him."

Tears welled in the older woman's eyes. "Damned old coot. I love him more than anything."

"I know you do." Reno swung onto Plenty Coups's back as soon as she was sure the cinch was tight.

"Let's go," Austin said.

He didn't have to tell her twice.

Reno took off at a full gallop. Her mind whirled as she thought about how proud Matt was, just like her grandpa Mel. And suddenly, Reno knew what her grandfather would've done in Matt's shoes.

She had a pretty good idea what the old cowboy was up to.

CADE SPOTTED THE HORSES first—Juker and the liver chestnut. Then he saw the familiar figure of Dakota Adair leaning over Matt, giving him CPR.

Dear God!

Bending forward in the saddle, Cade sent Jet flying across the ground, up the hillside. He pulled on the gelding's reins mere feet from his father, and was out of the saddle before Jet had come to a halt. "Dad!"

Dakota looked up. "I've got him breathing, but he needs help fast."

"Damn it, I don't have my cell phone!"

"Here." Dakota reached into his pocket. "I couldn't get a signal—didn't want to leave him. Maybe if you climb higher."

Feeling more helpless than he ever had in his life, Cade flipped the phone open. Sure enough, no service. Cursing, he scrambled up the mountain. Standing on top of a pile of boulders, he checked the phone again. *Finally.* Weak, but there was a signal.

His mom answered so quickly he knew she'd been sitting by the phone. "Cade, you're breaking up," she said. "Where…world…you at?"

"Is Austin there yet?" He knew the paramedics would already be on the way, but they needed a helicopter.

"He already rode out. Trent and J.T. are here."

"Let me talk to one of them." The deputies would know where to look; better than trying to explain to a 911 dispatcher over a fading cell signal.

Cade could hear several voices in the background as his mother took the cordless outside. Then J.T.'s voice nearly pierced his eardrum as the reception suddenly cleared. "We need Flight For Life," Cade said. "There's no other way to get Dad down the mountain fast enough." He explained as best he could where they were.

"Hang tight," J.T. said.

Heart pounding, Cade rushed back to where his dad lay.

Dakota was gone.

CHAPTER THIRTEEN

RENO STOOD BESIDE CADE until they heard the helicopter. "Go on," he said, waving her and Maura away. "That thing will spook the horses to kingdom come."

Reno scrambled into the saddle, and from the back of the palomino, Maura snatched up Jet's reins and Juker's, tugging the geldings along as they raced for the trees. They took cover while the medical copter landed in a clearing a short distance downhill from where Cade knelt at his father's side, and rescue workers poured out, running for Cade and Matt.

"How are they going to get him down there?" Maura shouted, before biting her lip.

"Stretcher," Reno called back over the noise from below. Horrified, she watched as they put Matthew in a scoop stretcher and carried him down the mountain to the waiting helicopter. Cade looked so forlorn standing there, watching the chopper take off with his father inside. Reno ached for him.

"Maura, can you please take Juker back to the ranch and stay with Estelle? I need a moment alone with Cade."

"Sure. Can you handle Jet, though?"

"I'll manage." With her right hand, Reno reached for the black gelding's reins. She was able to hold her roping rein with her left fingers while leading Jet beside Plenty Coups.

The noise of the helicopter faded away as she rode up beside Cade. She swung down from the saddle, handing him Jet's reins. "Are you okay?" *Stupid question.*

Without answering, he pulled her into a hug, burying his face against her shoulder. Their cowboy hats touched, Reno's nearly falling off. She righted it as he stepped back. His expression tore her up.

"I'm not ready for this," Cade said. "What the hell was Dad thinking?"

"That he wanted to die alone, with dignity," Reno said quietly.

Cade stared at her. "Why would he do that to my mom? Damn it, I didn't take him for the sort of coward to hurt her that way."

"I don't think that's what he meant to do." Reno stared intently at him. "Don't you understand? Your dad is dying by inches. What dignity is there in that? And why would he want to put your mother through the agony of watching him slip away slowly, in a hospital bed? He's a lot like Grandpa Mel." She lowered her gaze. "I believe that's what my mom did, too. She was ashamed of her weakness over Sonny, and she was already dying inside when she found out what he'd done." Reno swallowed. "I have the feeling that, deep down, she knew what Sonny was like long before he holed up in that shack. She couldn't live with herself and the pain she'd caused me and you."

"Caused *me?* You were the victim, Reno."

"Sonny had many victims. He made you take his life. He ruined mine—"

"Your life isn't ruined, Reno. You turned out fine."

She wanted to laugh—and cry. "Go home, Cade. Your mother needs you."

CADE WATCHED as his mom sat beside Matthew's hospital bed in the intensive care unit. Matt hadn't had a heart attack, thank God. Without his oxygen, he'd suffered something similar to an asthma attack. Lack of oxygen, combined with the high altitude, had made him pass out. Nevertheless, his prognosis was good. Cade also thanked the heavens above that his father had been discovered so fast. Now if only Cade could find Dakota and thank him, as well…

Matt's eyelids twitched as he finally woke up. He'd been asleep for the past hour and a half.

Estelle scooted her chair closer to his bed, but Cade hung back, giving them a moment. She reached to stroke Matthew's cheek. He brushed her hand away.

"Matt," Estelle said through tears, "what were you thinking?"

"What was *I* thinking? What were you thinking, woman? I went up on that mountain to die! Why'd you have to bring me down to this bloody hospital? This is exactly what I *did not want*."

Cade opened his mouth to speak, but his mom beat him to it.

"Don't you do that to me, Matthew," she sobbed, her voice rising. "Don't you dare rob me of one more day, or week, or even one more minute of life with you. You're not dead yet! And if you'd quit being so damn stubborn, you might be around for quite a while, which I'm actually crazy enough to want. Crazy enough to pray for." She took his hand in hers. "Can't you see how empty my life would be without you in it, you old cuss?"

Matt's blue eyes locked on hers, and his anger and defiance melted away. "I'm scared, Estelle," he said.

"I know. But I'm here, and I'll never leave your side."

Cade swallowed, despite the lump in his throat, and stepped to the other side of the bed. "Neither will I, Dad."

Matt managed a smile. He squeezed his wife's hand, reaching with the other for Cade's. Cade clasped his callused palm and felt his grip, still strong and firm. To his shock, Matt's shoulders began to shake.

"I love you both so much," he said. "I'm so sorry, darlin' Estelle."

"It's going to be all right." She wrapped her arms around him, hanging on for dear life.

Cade wiped away a tear, wishing his mom would never have to let his dad go.

"WANT SOME HOT COCOA?" Wynonna asked.

Reno turned from the kitchen window, where she'd been watching clouds scuttle across a full moon. "I didn't even hear you come in. I thought you'd gone to bed."

"I can't sleep," Wy said. "I'm worried about you."

"About me?" Reno made a face. "Pshaw, I'm fine. It's Matthew I'm worried about."

"You don't look fine," Wynonna said. She pulled out a kitchen chair. "Come on, sit down. Come on." She motioned with one hand, and Reno reluctantly sank into the seat. It was no use arguing.

Besides, Wynonna was right as usual. She wasn't fine.

"On second thought," the older woman said, startling Reno, "I think I left my bedroom light on." She made for the stairs.

"What?" Reno turned to look over her shoulder just as she heard a knock on the back door.

She got up to answer it and, through the window, saw Cade standing on the porch. She pulled the door open. "Is everything all right?"

"No." He thrust his hands into his pockets. "I was hoping you'd be home. Can I talk to you for a minute?"

"Is it your dad?"

"Dad's hanging in."

Reno opened the door wide. "Come in. Have a seat."

He pulled out a chair and sat at the table, one booted ankle crossed over the other. His face looked drawn and tired. "I want to know why you really left today."

"I had things to do."

"Reno."

"What?"

He reached across the table and took her hand in his. His grasp was strong, warm. He ran his thumb across her fingers, and the gesture gave her goose bumps. "I said something wrong."

"No, you didn't."

"I said your life wasn't ruined. But it was, wasn't it? At least, life as you'd always known it."

"I was a kid when I thought that. Kids are melo-dramatic. No biggie."

"You're not a kid now, and I know you're still

hurting." He held on tight when she would've pulled away. Then, half rising, he tugged her toward him. "Come here." He eased her onto his lap. "I wish I could wind back the clock, but I can't. Can we start over?"

Reno forced herself out of his lap, spinning to face him. "Cade…"

"Did I ever tell you my mom's dad was a cop?"

"What…? No." Where was he going with this?

"I never knew my grandfather. He got killed in the line of duty when Mom was thirteen. She was so proud of me when I became a lawman."

"I didn't know," Reno said. "Cade, what—"

"I could've just wounded Sonny." He stared, un-blinking, into her eyes. "Why couldn't I have been a better shot? Why did that bullet have to ricochet?"

"It wouldn't have made a difference," Reno said.

"It might've to your mother. Damn it, Reno, you say you understand why I shot Sonny."

"I do."

"Then forgive me."

"I already have. I told you—I never blamed you for killing him, or for what my mother chose to do. She didn't kill herself over Sonny's death, Cade. She gave up on herself after enabling Sonny's…what Sonny did when he was alive. She couldn't live with herself."

"That's not what I meant." He scraped his fingers across his chin. "Forgive me for leaving.

Let's start over, Reno." He stood. "Why can't we do that?"

Cade stepped toward her, but she pushed him away, not caring that it hurt her wrist. "Your dad may go downhill fast, or he may surprise everyone and live many more years. But either way, you'll leave. My *own father* left me after I was born. Then Sonny died, Mom killed herself and you left." Reno put her good hand against his chest and shoved again. "Well, guess what? I don't need you anymore, Cade. You had it right earlier. My life turned out just fine without you in it. Go take care of your mom."

"You don't mean that."

"Yes, I do!" She lowered her voice. Clenching her fists at her sides, she forced herself to calm down. "Leave, Cade. Now."

He turned and went out the back door, letting the screen bang shut behind him.

Reno fought the urge to go after him, and beg him to stay. But she wouldn't allow herself to do so. He had his life to live, and she had hers. She wasn't about to let him remain out of a sense of guilt.

She turned to see Wynonna standing in the kitchen doorway, sorrow on her face. "Are you all right?" the woman asked.

"I will be."

Wynonna walked over to Reno and gave her a

careful hug, cradling her head against her shoulder as though she were still a child.

"He's going to leave," Reno murmured. "I can't love him."

"Dear one," Wynonna said, smoothing back Reno's hair. "I think it's far too late for that."

CADE HAD TO FIND Dakota Adair. The guy had saved his dad's life. If Dakota was in some sort of trouble, maybe Cade could help. Plus, he still had the man's cell phone, which had rung more than once. He hadn't answered, not wanting to frighten the caller by having whoever it might be hear a strange voice.

Then again, maybe he should give the phone to Austin, even if it irked Cade to do it. The sheriff could check the caller ID, in case Dakota *was* involved in the poaching, and tracing the phone calls might lead to the horse thieves.

But poachers didn't go around committing good deeds....

Cade pocketed the cell phone. He would find Dakota first, talk to him, and then decide what to do. He owed the man that much.

Cade started by searching the area where he'd found his dad, where he'd last seen Dakota. It didn't take long to backtrack along the trail to where the truck with the black camper shell was parked— next to a black, three-horse, slant-load trailer.

Cade's stomach dropped as the horse trailer triggered a thought.

Black and silver.

A silver-blue truck with a black camper shell. Not a black and silver truck. Still…could this be the truck people in town had described, towing a horse trailer? Were Cade's instincts about Dakota wrong, after all?

Feeling the comforting weight of the .45 automatic he wore in his shoulder holster, Cade cautiously approached the campsite. The big Doberman came out from underneath the pickup and barked, baring its teeth. From around the far side of the horse trailer, Dakota appeared, leading his liver chestnut. The quarter horse was breathtaking, but Cade was only interested in the man holding her lead rope.

"Mornin'. Did you come here to shoot me?" Dakota asked, nodding toward the shoulder holster.

"I sure hope not," Cade said. "Is your dog going to eat me?"

"Chota." Dakota snapped his fingers, and the Dobie immediately dropped into a down position.

"He's well trained," Cade commented.

"He has to be," Dakota said, "as big as he is." His expression grew serious. "How's your dad?"

"Fine, thanks to you."

Dakota shrugged. "I only did what anyone would."

"If you hadn't had the cell phone…" Cade pulled it from his pocket and handed it to Dakota. "I came up here to thank you. And to ask you a couple of questions."

"What's that?"

"If you're here fishing and camping, wouldn't you be more comfortable at the KOA, where they've got running water and electrical hookups?"

"That's not my idea of camping out," Dakota said. "Besides, my dog doesn't like crowds."

Cade nodded. "Neither do I. It's just that… well…you might've heard about the poachers who are stealing mustangs in this area?"

Dakota laughed. "You think I'm one of them?"

"I don't know. Are you?"

"Not hardly. But I did have a run-in with a guy I believe was up to no good."

The hair on Cade's neck prickled. "What kind of a run-in?"

"On the last day of my permit, I did some fishing just before dusk. I had Chota with me. After I'd caught a couple of trout, I decided to stop at the watering hole and see if the mustangs were there. I like watching them."

"And?"

"And I saw some men on ATVs—three of them. A small band of horses had come to drink, and these men were trying to hustle them into a make-shift holding pen they'd set up with porta-panels."

Cade let out an expletive. "Why didn't you tell me this sooner?"

"Hey, can I finish my story?"

Cade pursed his lips. "Go on."

"When the men realized I'd spotted them, they started shooting at me." He reached to stroke the big Doberman's head. "Chota is a personal protection dog. He's had police-level training. He attacked one of the men. Bit down on the guy's arm, until he dropped his gun. He hollered something, and I called Chota off. I was afraid the others would shoot my dog. I, uh, pack a pistol of my own. For rattlesnakes and all."

Cade nodded.

"I shot back."

Cade's mouth dropped open.

"I didn't aim to hit anyone, just scare them. They all took off."

Cade stared at the other man for a long time before he asked, "Did you get a look at their faces?"

Dakota shook his head. "It was almost dark. But I *did* report them to the sheriff's office. One of the deputies took my written statement and a description of the ATVs, as best I could give him. One was painted camouflage, the other two were black or dark blue—I'm not sure. I was more worried about getting shot at, or having my dog get shot."

"Unbelievable." Cade folded his arms. "You were lucky." He thought of the night the poachers had fired at him and Reno. Either they were really bad shots, or they were only trying to scare the two of them—and now Dakota—away.

Why hadn't Sam mentioned the incident to him? Surely Austin had told him, even if he'd kept the info from Cade. For selfish reasons.

Macho jerk.

"So, tell me—how did you happen across my dad yesterday?"

"I've been hearing a mountain lion yowling the last few nights. And I spotted cat tracks near the creek bed yesterday, where I'd been fishing…before my permit expired." He pointed downhill to where a wide creek wound through the rocks. "The tracks led into the high country. I decided to ride up that way and see if I could spot the cougar. I didn't want it to get the mustangs, or my horse, either. I thought I'd report it to the game warden, but I wanted to pinpoint its location first. I took Chota out with me, and my revolver. That's when I spotted your father, lying on the ground."

"So, why did you ride away after you gave me your phone?"

The young man shrugged. "I didn't know what else I could do…. Besides, I…I had a feeling you were going to make a big deal out of what I'd done—and I'm no hero. Really. So I figured I'd get my phone back later."

Cade frowned. "If your fishing permit ran out, then why are you still camping here?"

"Long story." Dakota indicated an old-fashioned metal pot warming on a Coleman stove, circled by a ring of rocks. "Want some coffee?"

Wary, Cade swung down from the saddle. He was wearing his gun. Dakota didn't appear to be armed at the moment. Cade tethered Jet to the horse trailer, away from the mare. Dakota took another lawn chair from his camper shell and unfolded it, and Cade sat.

The coffee Dakota gave him smelled strong. Cowboy coffee. "I don't have any sugar," he said.

"I like mine black." Hiding his impatience, Cade blew on it, then cautiously took a sip. "So, why are you here, Dakota? You're not just camping, are you?"

The young man settled into the other folding chair, then took a deep breath. "When I found out about the poachers, I'm afraid I took it personally, especially when Reno's horses came up missing."

"What do you mean? And how do you know Reno?" *He couldn't.* She hadn't even seen Dakota up close, as far as Cade knew.

"I don't know her. Not yet. But she's the reason I'm in Eagle's Nest."

"Come again?"

"Nobody steals from my family and gets away with it," Dakota said. "Reno is my sister."

CHAPTER FOURTEEN

CADE NEARLY DROPPED his coffee mug. "Your sister? How can that be?" And then it hit him. Reno's biological father had left her mother after Reno was born. He could have other children.

"My mother…knew my father—Reno's father—when he was still married to Carlina."

Cade frowned. "But your last name is Adair, right?"

"Carlina used her maiden name again after she left my dad, and gave it to Reno. It took me a long while to find that out. And that she had remarried."

"To Sonny Sanchez," Cade said. "How did you find out all this?"

"I always knew my dad had been married before," Dakota replied. "I can't tell you how long I've been trying to piece it all together."

"So, he left Reno's mother and met—married?—your mom?"

"Carlina left *him*," Dakota stated. "Because my mom got pregnant—with me. So, yes, he married my mother after the divorce. My dad is Henry Adair. He never wanted Carlina to leave with his baby, but she was angry." He stirred the dirt with a stick, doodling. "Who could blame her? She took off when she was eight months pregnant."

"This was from Montana?"

"Yep. My father knew Carlina's parents lived in Colorado, and that they'd had a ranch, but he couldn't remember exactly where. He never spent much time there. Melvern Blackwell hadn't exactly welcomed him with open arms." Dakota looked up from his doodling. "Dad was a wild one, and Mel knew it. Plus, he and Carlina were so young. Seventeen, when they got married."

"How'd they meet, if your dad's from Montana?" Cade asked. Reno had never told him.

"At a powwow in Denver. They fell in love instantly. Or at least, Dad thought he was in love. At first Melvern wasn't about to let them get married. He threatened Dad with a shotgun." Dakota laughed wryly. "Told him to go back to Montana. And then Carlina's mother, Belle, found out she had breast cancer. Mel turned every bit of his attention to taking care of her. Carlina was heartbroken and Dad felt awful for her.

"Melvern finally gave in and let them be together, because Belle told him life was too short."

"Wow," Cade said. "I had no idea, and I know

Reno doesn't, either. So, Carlina and your father…fell out of love?"

"It's a long story—and my dad was as much at
fault as Carlina was—but, as I say, they were so
young."

"How did you finally find Reno in Eagle's Nest?"

"Internet. But initially that didn't turn up anything, because I was looking for Reno Adair. I
figured Carlina would've given her baby her father's—my father's—name, since she would've
been born before the divorce was final. Then one
day I saw an article in a horse magazine. It was
about Reno and her grandfather, Melvern Blackwell, and their mustang sanctuary here in Eagle's
Nest. I knew I'd found my sister. Melvern's not a
common name, plus Reno looks so much like our
dad, and the age was right. My mother—Sandy—
remembered Melvern quite well, since he was out
to skin my dad alive if he ever got ahold of him."
Dakota laughed without humor. "I can't blame him.
I'd feel the same way if I had a daughter."

"Carlina told Reno your dad abandoned them
right after Reno was born."

"I guess he deserted them, all right, any way you
look at it. He could've tried harder to find them."

"So, you're younger than Reno by…?"

"I'm twenty-six. My birthday is in December."

"Reno's is in February. You're ten months apart."
Cade studied the younger man. "Reno was nearly

twenty when that story was published in *Western Horseman*." Lord knew, he remembered reading it, too, still wallowing in guilt, with the shooting less than two years in the past. "And *Horse & Rider* printed an article on her and the sanctuary about a month ago."

"I saw it."

"Then why did you wait so long to come here looking for her?"

Dakota shrugged. "I was just a kid myself when I first found out where Reno was. But I'm here now."

"Yet you've been hiding out, camping…lurking around. You drove all this way. Why didn't you just go knock on her door?"

"And say what? 'Hi, I'm the brother you never knew about'?"

Cade sipped his coffee.

"I saw those men on their ATVs that night you and Reno shot at them. I was in my camper shell with my dog, getting ready to go to sleep. They drove by down below—didn't even look up and see me."

"I'll be damned."

Neither had Cade.

"I saw you and Reno, but then the bullets started flying."

Cade snorted. "Reno was doing the shooting, once they shot at us. She's a real spitfire."

"Runs in the family." Dakota grinned. "Anyway, I wasn't sure what was going on, but it wasn't hard to take a guess. I haven't seen them since that night."

"Reno saw you on her place a couple of days ago. What were you doing?"

"I cut across the BLM land and onto her land, thinking I'd finally just ride up and introduce myself. But I lost my nerve when she spotted me. Suddenly, I wasn't ready to face her at all." He shook his head, clearly disgusted with himself.

"Reno thought you were one of the poachers. She tried to catch you, but she lost your trail in the rocks."

"That was my intention."

"So, your dad—he's still in Montana?"

"Living outside of Big Timber. He's forty-five years old, still married to my mom. He wants to see Reno in the worst way, but he's afraid she'll hate him. That's why he's never tried to find her."

"Carlina lied to Reno. She thought her father didn't want her."

"Not hardly. Dad's never gotten over losing his daughter."

"Are you Apache, too?" Cade asked.

"No. Dad's Cherokee. So's my mother. She's originally from Oklahoma."

"Well, I'll be."

"Where do we go from here?" Dakota asked.

Cade polished off his mug of coffee. "I guess I need to introduce you to your sister."

RENO AWOKE FEELING TIRED and achy. She'd tossed and turned all night, and lay on her bad arm without realizing it. She realized it now.

After stripping off her clothes and wrapping her cast in a plastic garbage bag, she struggled to take a shower. She'd gotten fairly proficient at bathing one-handed, but hated the cast. She'd rather have her fingers smashed with a hammer than wear the damn thing one more day. *Still nearly four weeks to go.*

Downstairs, Wynonna had left a note, telling her she'd gone to the diner, and that homemade cinnamon rolls were wrapped and waiting on top of the stove. Reno peeled back the aluminum foil from the plate and inhaled. *Ah…nirvana.* The sweet rolls were still warm, thick with icing and cinnamon. She got a dessert plate from the cupboard and a glass for milk. She'd just picked up one of the sticky buns when the dogs began barking.

Reno moved to the window, roll in hand. "Crud." Cade knocked before she could get the frosting off her fingers. She was still licking at it as she hurried to the door, reaching gingerly to open it. Was he here to apologize again? "Cade—" Reno froze, speechless, her index finger halfway to her mouth.

A Native American, about her own age, stood on

the porch beside Cade, even taller than he was. From the description Cade had given her, he could be none other than the man from Larry's Boot Repair Shop—Dakota Adair.

What the hell was Cade doing with a suspected poacher?

Obviously, their suspicions had been wrong, or he wouldn't have brought him here.

"'Morning," Cade said, as though it was the most natural thing in the world for him to show up on her doorstep this way. As if they hadn't argued two days ago.

"Hello," Reno replied, addressing Cade's companion. She blinked.

"Reno, I'd like you to meet Dakota Adair. Have you got a few minutes?" Cade smiled briefly, staring at the frosting on her fingers.

"I—uh—sure." She wiped her hand on her jeans. *Nice manners, Reno.*

"Sorry," she said to Dakota. She held the door wide. "Come in." Cade wouldn't bring an outlaw into her house.

"What are you doing here?" she blurted.

Dakota grinned. "It's nice to meet you, too, Reno."

"Okay, I'm just going to dig a hole right now and drop through the floor," she said, her face red. "Apparently I left my manners in bed when I crawled out from under the covers this morning."

She went to the sink and washed her fingers, drying them on a dish towel. "Please forgive me, Dakota." She held out her hand. "The pleasure's mine." She narrowed her eyes. "But I still want to know what you were doing on my property the other day."

"Um, I think you two need to be alone for this," Cade said. "I'll be out on the porch." He strode toward the door.

Reno's mouth dropped. "Cade!" *What the hell?*

"I'll be right out here," he repeated, then closed the back door behind him.

"Um, have a seat?" Reno indicated a kitchen chair. "Do you drink coffee?" Wynonna had set the coffeemaker on auto-timer.

"Yes, thank you." Reno got two mugs down, forgoing her glass of milk. "Black's fine," Dakota added as she poured. He thanked her as, feeling a little like Alice down the rabbit hole, she set the coffee in front of him.

She tilted her head. "Just what *is* going on?"

"I don't know where to begin," Dakota said, cradling his mug in his hands. He took a deep breath. "This is a little awkward. More than a little, in fact."

"Just speak your mind."

"Reno, isn't my last name at all familiar to you?"

"Cade told me your name when he met you at the diner." She frowned, puzzled. "Should it be familiar?"

"Wow." He took off his cowboy hat and raked one hand through his long hair. "This is going to be even harder than I thought." Black hair. Like hers. And Wy's.

"You're family to Wynonna, aren't you?" she guessed. "I knew it. She's been looking for some of her cousins for a while now—"

"Reno, I don't know who Wynonna is. I came here looking for you."

"For me? I don't understand."

"Your father's been wanting to find you."

She froze. "My father? You mean my biological father?" She hesitated. "He sent you to find me?"

"He knows I'm here, but he didn't send me. I wanted to come. I've also wanted to meet you…for a long time now."

"Well, the suspense is killing me," Reno joked nervously. "My biological father left my mother and me. I honestly don't know his name. My mother never told me."

"Adair. Henry Adair."

And then it hit her. *Last name.* It would only matter if…

"My God." She clutched the table with both hands, completely forgetting her injury, and looked closer at Dakota's eyes. They were so like her own. Why hadn't she realized sooner? "You're his son, aren't you? You're my brother." She frowned. "No, that can't be right. You're a cousin?"

He fiddled with the edge of the tablecloth. "You had it right the first time, Reno. I'm sorry to spring this on you."

"Oh, Lord." She pressed her right hand to her chest.

Maybe she should've poured a shot of whiskey instead of a mug of coffee.

CADE WAITED ON THE PORCH, resisting the urge to eavesdrop. Truly, he felt as if he should take a walk out to the barn or something. Yet at the same time, brother or not, Dakota Adair was virtually a stranger. Cade wasn't about to leave Reno alone with him.

Wynonna chose that moment to drive up. Plastering on a smile, Cade got up from the wicker chair to greet her. "'Morning, Wynonna."

"Hey, cowboy. What brings you to my porch this early in the day?" She shouldered her oversize purse. "Is Reno still asleep?" She frowned. "Something's wrong. Is it your dad?"

"No, Dad's doing okay. He's being moved out of intensive care today. Matter of fact, I'm heading to the hospital to see him shortly. If all goes well, he'll be home this week."

"Well, that's a relief." Wy started up the steps. "So, what's happening?"

"You might not want to go in the house yet," Cade said. "Reno's talking to…someone."

"Who?"

"I think she'd better explain that to you. Trust me, just give her a few minutes."

Wynonna dropped into the rocking chair. "Now you've got me as curious as three cats. Cade, you can't leave me hanging like this."

Picking the right words, he said slowly, "You know the guy you and Reno saw…on the liver chestnut horse?"

"It's him—the guy from the boot shop?" Wynonna's eyes grew round. "But I thought you suspected him of being involved with the poachers?" She perched on the edge of the rocker. "Cade, what aren't you telling me?"

"The man's name is Dakota Adair. He's been trying to get up the nerve to come talk to Reno, because…" Her face had gone chalky. "Wynonna, are you all right?"

"You—you never told me his last name before. Henry—Reno's father—his last name was Adair."

"Yes." Cade bit his lip. He'd made a mess of this.

Wynonna slid back against the chair and began to rock, staring out into the distance. "It never occurred to me that Henry would have more children. I tried not to think about the bastard at all."

"He didn't leave Carlina," Cade said softly, feeling he should give Wynonna that much. "She left him."

"*What?* That's what he told you?" She gestured over her shoulder toward the door. "He's lying."

"I don't think so." Cade looked down at his feet. "I don't want to butt into Reno's business—this isn't for me to talk about. But for what it's worth, I believe the guy. And I think you will, too, if you give him a chance."

CHAPTER FIFTEEN

SHE HAD A BROTHER. Reno couldn't wrap her head around it. Any minute, she expected to wake up and find out Dakota Adair was nothing more than a figment of one of her vivid dreams.

She smiled as she put her truck in gear, turning out of her drive, heading toward town to pick up Maura to treat her to lunch. Even Wynonna had been smitten with Dakota's charm, Reno thought. The older woman was happy that Reno had family again—actual blood relatives. Reno had scolded her, reminding her *she* was family. But Reno had to admit it felt amazing to have a brother.

One who'd gone so far as to change his boot leather not to hide his footprints, as they'd originally thought, but to replace the soles with neoprene for better traction while he spent time in the wilderness watching the horses and waiting to meet Reno. That Dakota had driven all this way to meet her, and that he'd offered to help Cade and Sam keep a lookout over the herd, meant a lot to

Reno. "My brother," she said aloud. Two days since she'd met Dakota and she still loved the sound of the words on her tongue.

She looked at her watch. She couldn't believe she was here already. Reno pulled around to the back of Ted's Tack and Feed to the employees' entrance. And in one of their parking spaces, she saw a black-and-silver Ford truck, late seventies model.

Her pulse hammered.

Could this be the truck Cade had told her about? The thought had barely registered when Maura walked out the back door. "Hey, Reno," she said, leaning through the open passenger-side window. "I left my purse in Dad's truck. Duh." She rolled her eyes. "Be right back."

Reno watched as Maura walked over to the black-and-silver Ford, opened the door and got her purse. Her dad, Chet—a brand inspector. One who shopped for several hundred pounds of grain— more than a sheep rancher would need—not where Maura worked, but at the co-op.

Ridiculous. After all, Maura had said they had a couple of horses, too. And it was no crime to shop at the co-op; Reno herself did to get the best price. Just because Maura's dad didn't buy grain from the place where his daughter worked, didn't mean he was a poacher.

But he was a brand inspector. *How useful that*

would be in hauling horses across state lines, to have a brand inspector in the thieves' pockets.

"Okeydoke," Maura said, sliding into Reno's pickup. "What're you in the mood for?"

"Um…" Reno forced a smile, her appetite suddenly gone. "Anything. You name it and I'll claim it."

Maura laughed. "I'm hankering for a big ol' sub sandwich from Karl's."

"Karl's it is, then."

Reno drove on autopilot. Surely her friend wouldn't betray her. If Maura's dad was one of the poachers… Reno shuddered inwardly. She truly liked Maura. She'd been so kind to Reno, and so much help with the sanctuary. Her love for the mustangs was definitely genuine. Reno's suspicions must be wrong. Lots of people owned black-and-silver trucks. But Chet McPherson's had a fifth-wheel hitch in the back, for hauling a gooseneck trailer.

Another coincidence? Maybe.

Still, she made a mental note to tell Cade about it the first chance she got.

RENO WENT TO THE HOSPITAL after she dropped Maura back off at the feed store. She wasn't sure Cade would be there, but she wanted to pay Matthew a visit, anyway.

He was sitting up in bed when she knocked on

the open door to his third-floor room, Estelle in a chair beside him. "Hey, Matt, you're looking better." He was, too. He had some color back in his cheeks, though his breathing was still labored.

He waved her in. "I'd feel a heck of a lot better still if they'd let me out of this place."

Estelle got up. "It's nice of you to stop by, Reno. You just missed Cade."

"Oh. I was hoping to see him, too," she said. "Did he go back to the ranch?"

Estelle nodded. "He was planning to help Heath with some chores."

Reno slipped into a second chair, wedged between the bed and a curtained partition, staying long enough to give Estelle a lunch break, but not so long as to tire Matt. "So, when *are* they springing you from the joint?" she asked.

"In the morning," he said. "Hallelujah!"

"That's great."

Estelle returned in short order, and Reno rose and said her goodbyes. "Is it okay if I stop out at the ranch?"

"Of course." The older woman shrugged off her question. "You don't have to ask, Reno. You're always welcome."

"Thanks."

On the road again, Reno found her thoughts returning to the poachers. If Chet McPherson was one of them, then Austin or Sam Grainger ought to be able to make an arrest soon. Maybe they could get Chet to roll over on his partners in some sort of plea bargain. If he was involved, Reno wanted him to pay to the fullest extent of the law. But whatever it took to catch the other thieves…

She felt sorry for Maura if her hunch was true. She'd believed her own dad had betrayed her. To know he hadn't overwhelmed her.

"I need a little time to let this all soak in," Dakota had said the previous night. "And I'm sure you do, too, Reno. But I won't be far if you need me."

Reno was anxious to see the poachers arrested. Then she could focus on getting to know her brother. Maybe meet her father.

And forget she'd fallen back in love with Cade.

CADE FINISHED PUTTING OUT the last of the salt licks for the cattle. Heath had gone home a half hour ago, after the two of them had rounded up a few dry cows to take to auction. Heath would have to haul them to the sale barn, since Cade had his hands full.

Hot and tired, he wiped his forehead with the cuff of his denim shirt, then turned for the house. He'd just gotten out of the shower when he saw, through the small, fogged-up window, Reno's truck pull into the driveway. He should've expected her. After all, they had unfinished business.

She got out and came up the front walkway as

he tugged on some fresh clothes. He just had time to run his hands through his wet hair and open the door. "Hi, Reno," he said breathlessly. "Come on in."

"Thanks." She stepped into the living room, blinking as her eyes adjusted to the indoor light. "I wanted to come over and thank you for bringing Dakota to meet me."

He shrugged. "He would've talked to you sooner or later. He was just waiting to get up his nerve."

"Still, I'm glad you found him."

"Sit down?" Cade lowered himself on the couch beside her as Reno settled, leaning her cast on the arm of the couch. "How's the wrist?"

"Are we going to make small talk, or go ahead and acknowledge the elephant in the room?"

Cade pretended to check the corners. "I don't see one."

She shoved his knee. "That's the whole problem. Cade, I'm sorry I yelled at you about going back to Idaho. It did hurt me when you left, but, well, I guess I'm the one who's been ignoring the elephant. I know the past is in the past, and I also know you can't stay here in Eagle's Nest forever. I had no right to get mad at you over it."

"I hope you mean that," he said, running a hand through his damp hair again. "Because Mom and Dad and I had a talk this morning at the hospital."

"Oh?"

He let out a breath. "They've decided to sell the ranch," he said, "and come back to Idaho with me."

Reno looked stunned. "Wow. I never thought your dad would agree to that."

"Neither did I. Believe me, it took me by surprise—to say the least. But I have to admit, it also took a load off my shoulders. I wasn't looking forward to having to go back to New Meadows and leave Mom alone…with or without Dad." He wasn't looking forward to going back to Idaho no matter what, because that meant leaving Reno behind. But he had to put his parents first. He had no choice. They had no other family but him, and they couldn't keep their cattle ranch going.

At least Reno had Wynonna, and now her brother and father, from the way Dakota talked. But it didn't change how Cade felt about her.

"Well, at least you'll be here for a while yet," she said, attempting a smile. "I mean, it'll take time to sell the place. And even if you find a buyer right away, the paperwork will take at least a month or two, right?"

"I suppose." He felt like hell. The look on her face made him want to take her in his arms. He was already in love with her. "I still wish you'd come with me," he said. "There's plenty of room at my ranch."

Especially if you share my room…my life. Was he really up to taking such a big step? *Yes.* With her, yes. He'd marry Reno if she'd have him. Deep down, he'd always loved her. He'd simply been afraid to admit it, afraid to be anything at all like Sonny Sanchez.

But Reno was a grown woman now.

"I can't do that," she said. "I already told you, I'd never leave my mustangs, or Wild Horse Ranch. It was everything to Grandpa Mel. And then there's Wynonna…"

"You're right," he said. What had he been thinking? Reno and him as a married couple. *Right*.

Of course, he could always sell *his* ranch. But that would still mean having to help his mom take care of the Diamond L. And what new bride truly wanted to live with her in-laws, no matter whether it was here in Eagle's Nest or back home in New Meadows? Reno was her own person, a free spirit just like her mustangs.

His chest felt as if someone had hit him with a hammer. "This wasn't an easy choice," Cade said. The understatement resounded inside his mind.

"I'm sure it wasn't," Reno said. "Your parents have lived here for most of their married lives."

"That's not the choice I was talking about, Reno."

She wouldn't meet his gaze.

He looked at her cast. Austin's scrawled words jumped out at him. "So, you never did tell me— how'd your date with Pritchard go?" The thought that he'd be leaving Reno behind with that man lusting after her was enough to make him want to punch a hole in the wall.

"I canceled."

He raised his eyebrows. "Did you take a rain check?"

"Maybe."

He bristled.

You can't have your cake… He couldn't force Reno to love him.

"But the only reason I agreed to go out with him last night was to get out of a ticket."

Cade laughed aloud. He couldn't help himself. He would've loved to see the look on Pritchard's face when Reno reneged.

"That's not funny."

"I think it is."

She smacked at him with her good arm, and Cade caught it lightly, tugging her close. Before he could think twice, he was kissing her. At first she tensed, then slowly began to relax as he pulled her into his arms, still kissing her. Before he knew it, they were stretched out on the couch, and he was close to unbuttoning her shirt again. He thought about the red-and-black lacy bra she'd worn last time, and groaned.

"Whoa, hold up, Reno." He wasn't going to use her this way. He loved her. He couldn't make love to her, then turn around and leave when it came time to go home, since she'd made it clear that issue was what stood between them.

Cade sat up, helping her into a sitting position.

"You make me lose my mind," she said, glaring at him, flustered. She straightened her hair and put her cowboy hat back on. "I swear my brain turns to mush when you... Never mind."

He grinned. She *did* still care.

Maybe there was hope yet.

"At any rate, Mom and Dad could be home soon."

"Yeah," Reno said. "What were we thinking, making out like a couple of teenagers in your parents' living room?" She smiled, but her expression seemed sad, and it tore him up. Suddenly it wasn't funny at all.

"Besides, I need to go back to the hospital to help Mom bring Dad and all his stuff home." Matt had been deluged with cards, gifts and flowers from their friends and neighbors.

Reno stood. "I'm glad he gets to come home today."

"Me, too."

"Guess I'll see you later." She paused with her hand on the doorknob. "I almost forgot what I came over to tell you. Maura's dad, Chet McPherson, drives a black-and-silver Ford. I think it's a '78 or '79. It's got a fifth-wheel hitch, and Chet's a brand inspector."

Cade's stomach dropped. "I saw that truck at Mom's barbecue. Maura must've driven it that day."

"Do you think it means anything?"

"I sure hope not," he said. "I'd hate to think her dad was doing anything shady."

"I know. Maura and I have gotten to be close."

"Did you say anything to her, or to Austin?"

"No. I thought I'd tell you first. I'm going to call Sam Grainger, too."

"I can talk to Sam if you want. I'll be seeing him later today."

"I hope I'm not jumping to conclusions."

"It's worth looking into, that's for sure. I'll stop by Pritchard's office on my way to Sam's." It no longer mattered to him who caught the poachers, as long as they were arrested.

"Let me know what he says, all right?"

"I'll do that. Drive careful."

Cade walked her out onto the porch, watched her get in her truck and drive away.

If Chet McPherson was a crooked brand inspector, that would explain how the poachers were able to move the mustangs so easily, especially out of state.

Cade ducked back inside to grab his cowboy hat.

CHAPTER SIXTEEN

RENO DROVE BACK to Wild Horse Ranch feeling lower than silt in a creek bed.

You knew he would leave.

Tell that to her heart.

She'd known better than to fall in love with Cade, had promised herself she wouldn't let it happen. But she had. She'd fallen hard, as sure as the spill she'd taken from Cloud's back. She'd rather break her other wrist than feel this kind of pain. No amount of time would ever let her forget Cade.

About an hour later, Maura pulled into the driveway in her little S-10 pickup. Reno dreaded facing her friend, and hoped she could keep from giving anything away. She wanted Cade to have a chance to talk to Austin and Sam before she said anything to Maura about her dad.

She walked outside. "Hey, Maura. I thought you were driving your dad's truck today."

"I was, but when I got off work, he said he needed it."

For what? Hauling stolen mustangs? "So, are you ready to get a couple of our horses placed in a new home?"

"Yes and no." Maura tugged at her ponytail, tightening the band around it. "I'm happy if someone adopts them, but I've gotten attached to every one of them. I'll miss whichever ones go."

"I know the feeling." One thing Reno would bet on. If Chet was part of the poaching ring, Maura knew nothing about it.

Thirty minutes later, a couple in their mid-fifties showed up with their fourteen-year-old granddaughter to look at the horses. They liked Cloud, but Reno told them honestly that the gray was for experienced riders only, and gently nudged them toward a buckskin gelding and a sorrel mare. Both horses were in their mid-teens, with quite a few riding years left in them.

The couple agreed, and filled out the required paperwork. They promised to make arrangements to come back and pick the horses up, once Reno had the adoption approved by the BLM.

"They seemed nice," Maura said, after the three had left.

"It does my heart good," Reno replied. "A home for Buffy and Thunder means room for us to take in more horses." Lord knew, all the mustangs needed her right now. She prayed the poachers would be caught soon.

"I'm thirsty," she added. "Want a pop?"

"Sure," Maura said. "I'll get started on cleaning the paddocks."

"Be right back." Reno heard a truck arrive while she was in the kitchen, and when she went back outside, Austin's pickup was in the driveway. From a distance, she saw him talking to Maura.

Maybe he had news. Cade had probably talked to him by now. She'd have to find a way to get him alone. Reno hoped the sheriff wasn't here to question the girl about her father.

To her shock, as Reno walked toward the paddock, she saw Austin bracing both hands on the pipe railing on either side of Maura, pinning her between the fence and his tall frame. His shirt-sleeves were rolled up, showing off his tanned, muscular arms, and he was coming on to her. None too subtly, from the look of things!

Reno did a double take, then closed her mouth. She and Austin had never been exclusive, or agreed to anything serious. Still…

No wonder she distrusted people in general, men in particular. If Austin wanted to flirt with Maura, let him. Only, from the expression on her face, Maura was none too pleased with the attention. She looked as if she was trying to duck out from under his arm.

"Hey, Austin," Reno said. "What's up?"

He whirled around, then tried to hide his right

arm by his side, hastily reaching to roll down his sleeve.

But not before Reno saw the bite marks below his elbow. Bite marks that looked as if they'd come from the teeth of a very large dog. It was only then that she realized Maura's expression wasn't annoyance. It was fear. And the top button of her Western blouse was undone.

Reno froze in her tracks, cradling a can of pop in each hand. Tears welled in Maura's eyes, and Reno couldn't believe what she was seeing. Austin had always been grabby, but...

"Run, Reno!" Maura shouted. "Call Cade!"

"Shut up." To Reno's horror, Austin turned and backhanded her friend, knocking her to the ground before facing Reno. He climbed through the pipe railing. "I can explain the bites," he said.

It took a minute for what he'd said to register. *Bastard!* No-good, horse-thieving, woman-groping bastard! And he'd hit Maura.

Thoughts of Sonny overwhelmed her, and with all her might, Reno threw a can of pop at Austin, hitting him square in the forehead. Cursing, he stumbled backward, and she let fly with the second one, aiming for his groin. The can missed its target by inches, striking his thigh, but he cursed again and lunged for her.

Blue Dog flew out from beneath Reno's parked horse trailer. Growling low in her throat, she caught hold of Austin's pant leg and shook it like hunted prey. Tank had been lying near the paddock with Snap and Willow, and now the big white shepherd rushed toward them. Then he hesitated. He knew Austin, but he also sensed Reno's fear and fury.

"Get him!" she shouted. "Good girl, Blue Dog. Bite him, Tank. Sic him, Willow!"

Her panicked tone, combined with Blue Dog's actions, was enough to set the German shepherds on Austin, too. They grabbed and bit, tearing at his clothing. Even Snap joined the chaos, circling and barking, while Austin shouted at them and tried to get away.

Reno took the opportunity to reach in her pocket for her cell phone, as Wynonna ran from the house, armed with a broom.

"He's out at Reno's place," Deputy Carver told Cade.

Figures. "Thanks, J.T." Cade left the sheriff's office, and spotted Dakota coming from the diner down the street.

"Hi, Cade," the young cowboy called. "What's up?"

Cade filled him in on what Reno had said about the black-and-silver Ford.

"I've seen it," Dakota said.

"The sheriff's out at Reno's place. I was about to go over there to tell him."

"I'll drive," Dakota said. "I've got Chota with me."

The big Doberman was lying in the shade beneath the Chevy, and when Dakota whistled, he came out and jumped into the cab. "You're kidding, right?" Cade eyed the dog warily, stopping short of getting in with him.

Dakota grinned. "He won't bite you," he said. "Not unless you give him reason."

"Great." Cade climbed onto the seat as if he were sitting down beside a rattlesnake.

The dog leaned over to sniff his pant leg. "Easy there, big guy." *Don't sniff any farther north.*

"You can pet him," Dakota said, starting the truck's engine, switching on the air-conditioning.

Right.

Cade gave the dog a tentative pat, and to his surprise, the Dobie leaned into his touch, like a cat wanting a chin rub. Laying his head in Cade's lap, Chota rolled onto his side, turning partially over to expose his belly. He let out a sigh of contentment as Cade continued to scratch.

"Well, I'll be."

Dakota raised an eyebrow. "Told you. Dobies are big lapdogs at heart."

"Tell that to the poachers," Cade grunted. "Speaking of which, I need to call Sam." He dialed the number for the BLM office.

"Hey, Sam, it's Cade. I'm headed out to Reno's

place." He explained what she'd told him about Chet McPherson's truck.

"That's interesting," Sam said. "I never gave it a thought."

"Say, did you ever find anything out about the poacher with the dog bite? Did Austin get back any info from the hospital E.R.s?"

"Dog bite?" Sam sounded perplexed. "What dog bite?"

"The one Dakota Adair reported to the sheriff's office," Cade said. "You know, when the poachers shot at him and his dog?"

"Cade, I have no idea what you're talking about."

A sick feeling knotted Cade's stomach. "Pritchard didn't tell you?"

"No."

Shit. "I think you'd better get over to Reno's." He snapped the cell phone shut.

"What is it?" Dakota asked.

"He didn't know a thing about Chota biting the poacher."

"But I gave the deputy my statement," Dakota said. "I don't understand."

"I'm afraid I'm starting to," Cade muttered.

The deputy would've had to pass the report to Pritchard, which could only mean one thing.

Cade told himself not to jump to conclusions. Maybe it was the deputy who'd buried the information, not Austin.

Minutes later, they pulled up near Reno's barn and saw her dogs all over Sheriff Pritchard. Wynonna was hitting the man with a broom.

"What the hell?"

"That's him," Dakota said, slamming on the brakes. "The guy Chota bit. I didn't recognize him before, without his sheriff's uniform and cowboy hat."

Austin had climbed onto the upper rails of the paddock and was doing his best to kick and shake Reno's dogs off his legs.

Cade flung open the truck door, and felt the sharp scrape of Chota's toenails through his blue jeans as the Doberman sprang out.

Damn. He grabbed his thigh.

"Chota, watch him!" Dakota commanded.

Seeing the Doberman, Austin screamed.

Chota skidded to a halt just shy of the melee. Hackles raised, the dog obeyed his master, holding his stance while he barked and growled, eyes on Pritchard.

Austin reached for his pistol.

Chota leaped into the air, knocking him from the railing, teeth locked for the second time on Pritchard's gun arm.

Apparently the idiot hadn't learned much.

The next few chaotic seconds felt like an aeon. Reno took hold of Tank and Blue Dog's collars, Maura tugged on Willow's, and Snap darted in and out of the paddock, her staccato barking rising above the din of the other dogs. Wynonna continued to whack Pritchard with the broom, as Sam pulled up in his Bronco.

Everyone but Cade and Dakota were shouting. The two men reached for Austin at the same time, and Dakota twisted the sheriff's free arm behind his back.

"Call off your dog!" Austin hollered.

"Drop that gun and I will." Dakota's tone was surprisingly calm.

Personally, Cade wanted to let the dogs have Pritchard. In Cade's eyes, there weren't many things worse than a dirty cop. Except a child molester.

He grabbed Austin by the back of the shirt. Chota had let go on Dakota's command, and Cade yanked the sheriff away from dog and owner, throwing him roughly to the ground.

Before Austin could do more than squirm, Cade had a knee in his back. "Don't move," he said. "Or I'll let those dogs use you for a tug toy."

Austin froze, and Cade removed the sheriff's handcuffs from his belt and snapped them on his wrist, yanking Pritchard's other arm behind him to secure them. Sam moved in and took the man's keys, pocketed them and pulled him to his feet. Austin's cowboy hat had tumbled off in the scuffle, and he glared at Cade and Dakota, a purple-tinged goose egg already beginning to form in the middle of his forehead.

"I'm going to have all of you arrested for assaulting an officer!" he sputtered, looking wildly from one to the other of them, then back to the animals. "And your dogs put down."

"Oh, shut up," Reno said. "You make me sick. You're a disgrace to that badge you're wearing, and you're lucky these guys came along when they did."

He glared at her. "Yeah, talk big now that you've got help."

"I already had plenty of help," she retorted, still gripping Tank's collar. Blue Dog had calmed down somewhat. She was still growling, but more interested in sniffing noses with Chota than in attacking Austin. Wynonna crouched, broom at the ready, face pinched with anger.

Maura clung to Willow, shaking. Tears streamed down her face. "He tried to—to grope me—" she gulped, folding her arms over her breasts "—and when he did, I saw the marks where your dog had bit him." This last was to Dakota. Over lunch, Reno had told Maura about her brother and his dog, watching her friend's face as she described the way Chota had bitten one of the poachers.

Maura had looked stunned, but not guilty. Now Reno knew why. Austin was the culprit, not Maura's dad.

But…if a sheriff could go bad, so could a brand inspector.

"You ought to thank me," Pritchard said, spitting blood. Wynonna swung a mean broom.

"Thank you?" Reno clenched her fist, her temper flaring.

He grinned smugly. "Who do you think made sure your stolen horses were returned? I made them bring 'em back."

Reno narrowed her eyes. "That's supposed to make me feel better? That you so honorably returned them? I thought we were friends, Austin."

"We are. This was never about you, Reno. It wasn't personal."

Pathetic jackass. Cade had been right about him all along.

"Now that's where you're wrong. They're *all* my horses." Disgusted, she turned her back on him, and went to comfort Maura.

They heard sirens in the distance, and moments later, two squad cars came down the driveway.

"Looks like your ride's here," Sam said, shoving Austin forward.

J. T. Carver and Trent Jackson got out of their vehicles and met them halfway.

"Sheriff Pritchard?" J.T. stared, unable to believe his eyes.

Austin said nothing.

CHAPTER SEVENTEEN

IT HADN'T TAKEN LONG for Austin to throw his cohorts under the bus. He knew the art of plea bargaining. Chet McPherson had written up phony brand inspection slips for the horses Austin, Chet and the third poacher, Chet's nephew, Jake, had stolen, since brand inspections were legally needed to sell a horse.

Austin, it turned out, had lost a lot of money on Internet gambling, and at the racetrack. He and Chet—both horse racing aficionados—had run into a friend of Chet's at the track, a man named Murphy who worked on a dude ranch in California.

He and the other two devised a plan to catch as many mustangs as they could, dump the old ones off to killer buyers, and sell the rest to the dude ranch owner Murphy worked for. Murphy would break and train them in exchange for a cut of the profits.

"Reno, I swear I didn't know anything about

what they were doing," Maura sobbed, the day after Austin and the others had been arrested. She sat on Reno's porch with her, Cade, Wynonna and Dakota. "I can't believe my dad would do such a thing, and that Jake would help him. I'm so ashamed."

"Don't cry, Maura," Wynonna said. "We know *your* heart is good." She handed her a tissue.

"My mother is so embarrassed, she wants to sell our ranch and move away." Maura dabbed at her eyes. "But I'm staying, no matter what she does. I'll find a roommate to live with…or something."

"I think we have a spare bedroom you can use if you need to," Reno said, giving her friend a hug. "Right, Wynonna?"

"Absolutely."

"Do you have a parking spot for a brother's truck and trailer?" Dakota teased. "Because I called Dad, and he's flying out here to pay a visit as soon as he can get a plane ticket." His eyes sparkled.

"Don't be silly," Reno said. "Do you think I'd let my family sleep out in the driveway? This house has four bedrooms. And a stall for your horse while you're here, and room for your dog."

"Thanks," Dakota murmured. "I appreciate it."

"Looks like everyone is selling their ranches," Wynonna said.

"Oh?" Reno raised her eyebrows.

"Cade's parents are putting the Diamond L on the market. I thought you knew." She glanced apologetically at Cade. "They're going back to Idaho with you, right?"

"It appears that way," he replied, his playful mood gone. "They'll have to talk to a Realtor…all of that fun stuff." He didn't meet Reno's gaze.

She bit her lip and told herself she wouldn't cry like Maura. The poachers were behind bars, and she'd found a brother and her real father. That mattered.

"Say, how would you and Maura like to come out to the barn with me and figure out where Dakota's going to keep his mare?" Wynonna asked.

Dakota looked puzzled. "I didn't know you were into horses, Wynonna. Reno said—"

Maura elbowed him in the ribs. "Wy helps out on occasion," she said pointedly.

"Yeah. I'm not just good in the kitchen, I'm good in the barn." Wy tucked her arm through his as she tugged Dakota to his feet. "Too bad you're family, Mr. Tall, Dark and Handsome."

Dakota laughed. "Lead the way. But no hay-lofts." He smiled at Reno over his shoulder. "I hope I'll be safe with these two wild women."

"You're in good hands," Reno said.

She watched the three walk away, knowing Wynonna meant well in trying to give her time alone with Cade. She just wasn't sure she had anything more to say to him.

"You certain you won't take me up on my invitation to move to Idaho?" Cade asked.

Reno swallowed over the lump in her throat. "I already told you, I can't."

He dragged his chair closer to hers. "It's not Idaho standing in our way, Reno. It's you."

"What?" Reno's jaw dropped. "Have you gone loco?" She gripped the arms of her rocking chair to keep her hands from shaking. "What are you saying?"

"You always have to be in control, don't you? Because of the past, you won't allow yourself to turn loose and let *me* take control—me or anyone else." He stood, then leaned in and kissed her. "I promised Mom I'd be home in time for supper, but I'll be back later."

Reno trembled. "You *are* crazy, Cade, you know that?"

He only waved at her over his shoulder, without looking back.

Reno waited until he'd driven away to give in to her tears. Things were so much simpler before Cade had come back to Colorado.

And so much less wonderful.

Reno looked up at the sky. "Are you watching, Grandfather? I'm sorry about Storm-Bringer." Just as she'd feared, the poachers had been selling the old horses to killer buyers. Reno couldn't bear the thought. She wished the law still hanged horse thieves. "But I'm never leaving this ranch, not until the day I die. I'll take good care of your horses."

Reno closed her eyes and said a prayer, and when she looked up, Dakota was headed back from the barn with Maura and Wynonna.

"Where's Cade?" Wy asked.

"He went home. Said he'd be back later."

"Keep your chin up," she murmured sympathetically. "He's not gone yet."

"I thought you said he went home." Dakota frowned, puzzled, and Maura elbowed him in the ribs again. "Ow! Would you stop that?"

"Only if you let me ride that pretty horse of yours."

He grinned. "I'm going to pick Feather up right now. Want to ride along?" He'd left his horse and trailer at his campsite, the liver chestnut in a portable corral with Chota on guard.

"Love to." Maura smiled, her eyes still a little puffy.

"I'll have dinner on the table by the time you get back," Wynonna said. "I hope you like enchiladas."

"Are you kidding?" Maura smacked her lips. "They're my favorite."

"You okay, girl?" Wynonna asked after the other two left.

"I will be," Reno said, squeezing Wy's hand. "I'm a pretty lucky woman."

"I'll say. Well, I'm going to get the enchiladas started." She disappeared through the kitchen door.

Reno sat alone on the porch, barefoot, lost in thought.

She was still daydreaming when Dakota and Maura returned, hauling the black three-horse trailer. Reno ducked inside the house and grabbed her socks and boots. She wanted to see Feather up close. The mare was breathtaking.

By the time she got outside, Dakota already had the liver chestnut unloaded. Maura stood in the yard, holding Feather's lead rope, while Dakota walked around to the back of the trailer. What was he doing? Maybe getting his tack? It would be easier to drive closer to the barn to unload it.

Reno started down the stairs, opening her mouth to call out. Instead, she gasped as he led a second horse out of the trailer.

A coal-black mare with a lightning-bolt blaze on her face.

"Storm!" Reno ran toward them, slowing as she got closer, in case she spooked the mustang. "Where did you find her?" She approached cautiously, speaking softly to the mare. "And how did you get her to load? To lead, even?"

"Cade found her," Dakota said. "I guess the poachers thought she was pretty enough to hang on to, even if she is old. They had her in a holding pen hidden near the canyon. Cade wanted to surprise you."

And how.

Reno pressed her fingers to her lips. "How did you get her into the trailer?" she repeated.

"We got a little help from Dr. Russell," Maura explained. "He gave her a tranquilizer to calm her enough to get her in. Said to tell you he should come float her teeth before you turn her back out with the herd. He's pretty sure she's over twenty, but said she's in really good shape for her age."

"She must've been taught to lead at some point in her life," Dakota said. "She's a little jumpy, but she didn't seem to mind when I put the halter on her. We had to run her into a makeshift squeeze chute to tranq her."

"I don't remember exactly when my grandfather first saw her with the herd," Reno said. "But I know she wasn't a foal. I think she was a yearling. Maybe she escaped from someone's ranch back in the day."

"Could be. She looks part quarter horse."

Reno stroked the mare's neck. Goose bumps ran up her arms, to be actually touching the horse her grandfather had named, and had loved for so many years.

"Poor old thing," Maura said. "Can't she just stay here at the sanctuary?"

"She could," Reno said, "but I don't think she'll be happy penned up." Cade and Sam Grainger had recovered the better part of the mustang herd Austin had stolen, including the stallion Reno called Windchaser, and the bachelor band of young colts. Sam had contacted the BLM office in California, and the agents there planned to go to the dude ranch where

Murphy worked, and confiscate any horses that had been illegally obtained.

More of her herd could be coming home soon.

AFTER DINNER, when the dishes were done, Dakota asked Maura to take a walk with him and Chota.

"I'll have your room ready by the time you get back, Dakota," Wynonna promised.

"Thank you, Wy. Reno. For everything."

Maura gave them each a hug. "Most people in your position wouldn't be so nice to me."

"Get out of here," Reno said, "before I put you back to work."

She watched her tall, strong brother walk away with Maura, cute and tiny, at his side.

"I think he likes her," Wynonna said.

"I believe the feeling is mutual." Reno sobered. "Alone again…" She sighed. "Don't ever leave me, Wy."

Wynonna gave Reno's knee a pat. "Go on, you. I'm going to make up his room, then I'm going to bed to curl up with my book."

"I'll do the room," Reno said.

"No. You've still got over three weeks until you get your cast off, and you've been overdoing, to say the least."

"Feels more like three months," Reno said.

"Don't whine. Hey, you can sure sling a mean pop can. I'll bet Sheriff Pritchard's still trying to remember his own name. You hit him right in the head."

"*You* clobbered him pretty good with that broom." Reno still found it hard to believe the man she'd thought was her friend—her boyfriend at one time—had turned out to be a traitor.

And Cade wondered why she had trust issues.

It was dusk when Reno sat back in the rocker and propped her boots on the porch rail. She heard a truck, and her heart picked up a beat. Sure enough, it was Cade.

He parked and sauntered over, handsome as always. In that moment, Reno thought she could watch him every day and never grow tired of doing so. His cologne tickled her senses as he drew near. He wore the black Western shirt he looked so sexy in, with his new boots and a faded pair of jeans. His hair was damp beneath his cowboy hat, so he must have had a shower. He still needed a haircut, but the look was growing on Reno.

"How's your dad doing?" she asked.

"Not too bad." Cade sat in the chair beside her.

Reno swallowed. "Did you and your parents get everything worked out?"

"Yep."

Did she have to pull every word from the guy?

"It looks like I'm going to have to go back to Idaho sooner than I'd expected," Cade said.

Her stomach roiled. "Why's that?"

"Because it's awful hard to put your ranch up for sale when you're a thousand miles away."

It took a minute for what he'd said to register. "Put your ranch… But I thought your parents were selling the Diamond L. And going back to Idaho with you?"

"They can't."

"Why? Is your dad too sick to make the trip?" She hadn't thought of that.

"No. They can't go because they wouldn't have anywhere to live."

Reno's heart jumped.

"I told you. I'm selling my ranch." He reached out and took her hand, tugging her into his lap. "I had another long talk with Mom and Dad tonight. They understood why I decided to sell. They were relieved, since Dad didn't really want to move, anyway. And with the money I'll get from my place, I can help them pay off their debts and then some."

"I'm glad, Cade. They need you." *So did she.*

"And I need *you*," he said. "Didn't I tell you to trust me?"

She looked down, ashamed, but he reached out and lifted her chin. "There's no way I could leave Eagle's Nest again. Not if it means leaving you behind."

Reno's heart soared. "You better not be messing with my head, Cade Lantana. I'll have my brother kick your butt. Or sic his dog on you."

"I'm not afraid of your brother," he said. "Chota…well, maybe." He kissed her. "Just don't throw any pop cans at me."

Reno kissed him back. "So, you're going to live at the Diamond L?"

"For a short while," he said. "Mom and Dad have decided to sell most of the cows and turn the place into a guest ranch." Reno reached up and tipped his hat to better see his eyes—make sure she'd heard him right, and that he wasn't messing with her. Her heart soared.

"Really? That's a great idea. Your mom will have company all the time, and it'll give your dad something fun to do to keep from being bored. He's a great storyteller. The guests will love him."

"That they will," Cade agreed. "Plus, having a guest ranch will mean a solid income for Mom and Dad. It'll give her something to fall back on when…" His expression grew wistful. "Well, anyway, I don't know why I didn't think of the idea myself. I'll bring my horses out here, because I still want to raise cutting horses. Besides, we'll need some for the guests to ride, and Mom's going to keep a few cows around for them to putter with."

"I think they made a movie about that," Reno teased.

"Actually, Dad would make a pretty good Curly," Cade said. "Old and crotchety. Just like in City Slickers."

"Better not let him hear you say that."

"You're right. He might have a lot of years ahead. He's liable to live long enough to teach his grandchildren a thing or two."

"Grandchildren?" Reno asked. "Don't you need a wife for that?"

"Oh, I don't know." Cade rubbed his chin. "I was thinking about maybe getting a harem of cowgirls to move onto the ranch." He ducked, but not quite fast enough, and she smacked his shoulder good and hard. "Ow."

"I don't think so."

"Is that right?" He smiled. "Does that mean you're going to marry me?"

Reno nearly lost her breath. "Does that mean you're going to ask me to?"

He kissed her until she felt dizzy. "Yes, I'm asking," he said, when they finally came up for air. "Reno Blackwell, will you change your name to mine?"

"I don't know. Having two Cades in the family might be confusing."

"I love you, silly woman."

"I love you, too, you mean ol' thing. You scared me, you know."

"Scared you? How?"

"The way you were going on earlier, I thought you really were leaving for Idaho."

"Why, Reno, I didn't think you were scared of

anything." He threw her own words back at her, from the day when she'd first teased him about Chota. "A tough Apache-Cherokee cowgirl like you doesn't run, which is good, since I wanted to catch you."

"It's about time," Reno said. "Hey, that's right. I am half-Cherokee, aren't I?" She grinned. "And I have a dad and a brother."

"I'm so glad you brought that up." Cade stood, holding her hand. "Let's go for a drive. I have a surprise for you."

"CLOSE YOUR EYES," Cade said, as they drove down the narrow gravel lane that led to a little fishing cabin.

She did, putting her hand over them. "Where are you taking me?"

"Trust me?"

"I'm working on it."

He chuckled. "I love your honesty." He turned off the ignition once he'd parked. "Keep your eyes closed. I'll be around to help you out."

For once, she didn't protest. Opening the passenger door, Cade reached inside and took her by the elbow. "No peeking."

Breathing in the scents of pine and spruce, she asked, "How am I supposed to walk?"

"I'll lead you."

He turned the key and opened the cabin door,

then flipped on the light switch. "Okay, you can open your eyes now."

Reno lowered her hand, still standing on the front stoop. Her smile widened as she took in the cabin, the trees and wildflowers surrounding it.

"What's this?" she asked, stepping through the door.

"I rented it for a few days. I wanted to have it all fixed up with lit candles and all that romantic stuff you see in the movies, but, well, the truth is, Reno, I couldn't wait one more day, one more minute, to be with you."

"Really? And what if I would've said no?"

"I would've spent the weekend fishing. There's eighteen-inch rainbow trout in the stream out back, did you know that?"

She shoved him. He grabbed her and, kicking the door shut, walked her backward toward the bed. "You still haven't officially said yes," he reminded her, removing her hat before pressing her gently down onto the bed.

Reno lay on her back, her hair fanned out around her. Cade ran his fingers through it, reveling in the silky texture and the way her dark eyes sparkled in the dim light.

"How'd you get the lamps on?" Reno asked.

"Wall switch." He kissed her. "Well?"

"I'm impressed," she said. "I didn't think a rustic cabin like this would have electricity."

He tickled her and she shrieked. "Stop!"

"Say yes."

"Yes!" Reno wriggled and twisted beneath him, and he loved every minute of it. Loved playing with her, as if they were kids again.

"Yes, you'll marry me?"

"Yes, Cade." She wrapped her arms around his neck. "I'll marry you."

"Good, because I'd hate to have to take this back to the jeweler." He unsnapped the pocket of his shirt and took out the diamond ring he'd been carrying around for two days now—a modest, pear-shaped stone set in white gold.

Reno gasped as he slipped it on her finger. "How did you…get my size? Wynonna knows!"

He grinned.

Reno pulled him against her. "Come here, cow-boy."

He kissed her mouth, then began to undress her, starting with her boots. He wanted to rush—every hormone in his body was screaming at him. But at the same time, he wanted to take this slowly. Making love to Reno was something he'd waited for a long, long time.

"I've been such a fool," he said. "I never should've left Colorado, never left you, Reno."

"Shh. The past is just that, remember?"

"Don't ever let me forget." He slipped her T-shirt over her head, then unhooked her bra. This one was blue, and looked fabulous on—and off—her. Cade drank in the sight of Reno's breasts, her creamy brown skin…her nipples dark, erect. "I love you," he said, caressing her. "I'll always love you, Reno."

"You'd better," she said. "Because I love you, too, Cade." She slid her hands over his chest and unsnapped his shirt.

He also loved the way his ring looked on her finger. Soon, she'd be wearing the matching wedding band. Soon, she'd be his wife—officially. Tonight he planned to make her his wife in every way that really mattered. In his heart, in his mind, and with the joining of their bodies.

Cade shrugged out of the shirt and tossed it on the floor, along with his hat. Reno gasped. "That's a 10X beaver."

"It's built to take it," he murmured against her mouth as he reached to unbutton her jeans. He slid the zipper down, and she did the same to his, revealing the one thing he'd never thought he'd wear for anyone.

"Sexy black briefs." Reno's eyes widened. "Who would've thought?"

He eyeballed her baby-blue thong. "And how."

In seconds, they were naked between the soft, cotton sheets. Cade kicked the comforter onto the floor. They wouldn't need it. He brushed his erection against Reno's inner thigh, and she moaned.

"If I'm dreaming, don't wake me up."

"You are my dream," he said. "My dream come true." He kissed her breasts, licking her nipples, taking them into his mouth in turn. He explored every inch of Reno's body, kissing her curves, all the way to the arch of her foot and back up again.

Together they teased and tasted each other, until Cade thought his brain would explode. He paused long enough to put on a condom.

"You did come prepared," Reno breathed.

"For now," he said. "But later I want babies. Lots of babies."

"Mmm, I think we should practice first. For a really, really long time."

"You've got it." Slowly, he entered her, pushing into her warm sweetness.

She gasped, grabbing his thighs, running her hands over his backside as she pulled him closer. Cade moaned against her mouth.

Deep down, he had never wanted anyone but Reno. He'd been alone a long time, and the wait for her had been worth it. He felt as if she was his first.

And in a way, she was. His first real love.

They climaxed almost simultaneously, and Cade buried his face against her neck, nibbling kisses across her throat, her earlobes, her jaw. "I love you so much."

She kissed him back, nipping his shoulder, exciting him all over again. "I love you more," she said. "I've never felt like this before, Cade."

He rolled over and pulled her on top of him. "Let's see if I can make you feel even better."

Slowly, tenderly, he showed her all over again how much he loved her. Then, with the dim lamplight still spilling across their entwined bodies, she fell asleep in his arms.

CHAPTER EIGHTEEN

WHEN RENO'S CAST CAME OFF, she had to work at getting her arm back to normal. Following her doctor's instructions, she lifted one-pound, then two-pound weights, and used a hand grip to strengthen and exercise the muscles in her wrist and fingers. At the end of August, all eyes would be on her left hand as Cade slipped on a wedding band.

"The diamond looks better without the cast," he decided as Reno sat on the front porch, working her grip.

"I don't know. I was sort of getting attached to the neon green. Maybe a matching wedding gown…?"

"Reno, I'd marry you in a purple tuxedo, if that's what you asked me to do."

"Keep that attitude," she said. "I like it."

"I have something you'll like even better." He laid a folded piece of paper on her lap.

"What is this?" She opened it and saw a phone number.

"Dial it."

She raised an eyebrow. "Who's going to answer?"

"Dial it and see."

Reno picked up her cell phone. On the other end, country music greeted her, then a man's voice said, "Hello, Reno. Are you ready to walk your old dad down the aisle?"

"Henry." Reno smiled up at Cade.

"I thought you were supposed to walk *me* down the aisle," Reno said into the phone. She'd only known him for a few weeks, but she was looking forward to getting much closer.

"I don't know. I'm getting up there in age. You may have to walk me."

She laughed. "You're forty-five."

"That's a lot in dog years." It turned out Henry loved dogs, too. He was a professional trainer and had twelve dogs of his own, including Chota's dam.

"You're nuts," Reno said.

"Runs in the family. So, are you ready for the big day?"

"I'm picking up my dress tomorrow."

"That won't be necessary." Henry's voice echoed in stereo as he walked around the corner of the house and stepped up onto the porch, a garment bag draped over his arm. Laugh lines creased the corners of his eyes.

Reno dropped the phone and jumped up. He

closed his cell phone and held his arms open. Tall like Dakota, Henry was a handsome man. His thick hair had very little gray, and he wore it cut short beneath a silver cowboy hat.

Reno moved into his embrace, squeezing him tightly. It felt so strange to hug her father, yet so right.

"Don't let Cade see." Henry's eyes crinkled as he held out the dress.

"Thank you," Reno said. "But you shouldn't have picked it up. It wasn't paid for yet."

"It is now."

She hugged him again. "You shouldn't have."

"Why not? A man's daughter only gets married once. At least, it better be once." He gave Cade a stern look.

"If I have anything to say about it, it will be," Cade promised.

THEY HELD THE WEDDING on the last Saturday of August. Dakota looked sharp in his black Western tuxedo and cowboy hat, standing up beside Cade as his best man. Wynonna was Reno's matron of honor, Maura her bridesmaid.

If Dakota looked sharp, Cade looked stunning. He took Reno's breath away as she slipped her arm through the crook of Henry's elbow and walked to meet her groom.

The ceremony was outdoors, near the riverbank

where the mustangs roamed. The guests had all brought folding chairs, setting them up on whatever level spots were available. They'd opted to let Mother Nature do the decorating, the wedding party gathered beneath a stand of evergreens. The tall mountain grasses of late summer swayed in the breeze around them, a scattering of late-blooming wildflowers sprinkled here and there.

The sound of the river rushing past served as their music as Reno stood beside Cade. His own black, Western tux was custom fit, his white dress shirt made of silk. He'd worn his good hat and his Tony Lama boots.

Wynonna and Maura wore lilac, Cherokee Tear dresses that Wy had made, with white cowboy boots on their feet.

Reno wore white lace-up boots, ankle high— old-fashioned to match her dress. Her wedding gown was simple yet elegant, with sheer lace sleeves, a full skirt and modest train. It nipped in at the waist, with a row of covered buttons running all the way up to the delicate lace at her throat. The look on Cade's face as he stared at her was worth every dollar the dress had cost.

Henry stood with her in front of the podium the Cherokee preacher had set up between twin towering pines.

"Who presents this woman to her man?" the minister asked.

"I do." Henry patted her hand, still tucked through his elbow. "I give my daughter to be married to this man."

Reno stood on tiptoe and kissed him on the cheek. "Thank you. I love you, Dad."

Henry's eyes glistened, and he nodded to Cade as he placed Reno's hand in his son-in-law's.

Reno held her small bouquet of wildflowers in her right hand, gripping Cade's hand with her left.

"Friends, family, we are gathered today in the glory of God and our Mother Earth and Father Sky, to unite these two people in holy matrimony. It is a state of living not to be taken lightly or thoughtlessly. A way of life to share for eternity, two people coming together as one. For God has said a man shall leave his mother and father and join his wife in marriage."

Out of the corner of her eye, Reno saw Wynonna dabbing her eyes with a powder-blue handkerchief. She knew that Matt and Estelle, who sat behind and to the left of Cade, were equally moved. She'd seen a tear in the old cowboy's eyes when her father walked her past her father-in-law. And Estelle had worn waterproof mascara for a reason.

"Cade, do you take Reno to be your wife? To love and cherish her for all the days you shall live? To treat her with honor and grace?"

"I do."

"And, Reno, do you take Cade to be your husband? To love and cherish him for all the days you shall live? To treat him with honor and grace?"

"I do."

"Then let no man destroy what God has brought together. Let nothing come between these two people, who have professed their love today before us all. The rings?" The preacher held out his hand, and Dakota put the wedding bands in his palm. The Cherokee man held them to the sky, facing in turn the four directions. "Let these rings represent the full circle of life. It is the way of the Cherokee people, the way of life itself. For everything has a beginning and an end that forms an unbroken circle."

Cade slipped the white-gold band on Reno's finger, and she did the same with his ring.

"By the power given to me through God and Christ Jesus, I pronounce you husband and wife. You may kiss the bride."

And kiss her he did. Then the preacher held his hands aloft, toward the onlookers.

"Ladies and gentlemen, I present to you Cade and Reno Lantana."

"Throw the bouquet!" someone shouted.

Reno laughed, and once the single women had lined up, turned her back to them, and tossed the flowers over her shoulder. She spun around and looked right at Wynonna, who held her prize high above her head.

Barry Biltmore caught Wynonna's eye and gave her a wink.

Reno smiled.

Love was definitely in the air today.

Her spirit soared as the crowd cheered and whistled. The joyous sounds rang across the mountains as she stood beside her husband, the man she loved with everything she had.

* * * * *

Here is a sneak preview of
A STONE CREEK CHRISTMAS,
the latest in Linda Lael Miller's acclaimed
McKETTRICK *series.*

A lonely horse brought vet Olivia O'Ballivan to Tanner Quinn's farm, but it's the
rancher's love that might cause her to stay.

A STONE CREEK CHRISTMAS
Available December 2008
from Silhouette Special Edition

Tanner heard the rig roll in around sunset. Smiling, he wandered to the window. Watched as Olivia O'Ballivan climbed out of her Suburban, flung one defiant glance toward the house and started for the barn, the golden retriever trotting along behind her.

Taking his coat and hat down from the peg next to the back door, he put them on and went outside. He was used to being alone, even liked it, but keeping company with Doc O'Ballivan, bristly though she sometimes was, would provide a welcome diversion.

He gave her time to reach the horse Butterpie's stall, then walked into the barn.

The golden retriever came to greet him, all wagging tail and melting brown eyes, and he bent to stroke her soft, sturdy back. "Hey, there, dog," he said.

Sure enough, Olivia was in the stall, brushing Butterpie down and talking to her in a soft, soothing voice that touched something private inside Tanner and made him want to turn on one heel and beat it back to the house.

He'd be damned if he'd do it, though.

This was *his* ranch, *his* barn. Well-intentioned as she was, *Olivia* was the trespasser here, not him.

"She's still very upset," Olivia told him, without turning to look at him or slowing down with the brush.

Shiloh, always an easy horse to get along with, stood contentedly in his own stall, munching away on the feed Tanner had given him earlier. Butterpie, he noted, hadn't touched her supper as far as he could tell.

"Do you know anything at all about horses, Mr. Quinn?" Olivia asked.

He leaned against the stall door, the way he had the day before, and grinned. He'd practically been raised on horseback; he and Tessa had grown up on their grandmother's farm in the Texas hill country, after their folks divorced and went their separate ways, both of them too busy to bother with a couple of kids. "A few things," he said. "And I mean to call

you Olivia, so you might as well return the favor
and address me by my first name."

He watched as she took that in, dealt with it,
decided on an approach. He'd have to wait and see
what that turned out to be, but he didn't mind. It
was a pleasure just watching Olivia O'Ballivan
grooming a horse.

"All right, *Tanner,*" she said. "This barn is a
disgrace. When are you going to have the roof
fixed? If it snows again, the hay will get wet and
probably mold…"

He chuckled, shifted a little. He'd have a crew out
there the following Monday morning to replace the
roof and shore up the walls—he'd made the arrangements over a week before—but he felt no particular
compunction to explain that. He was enjoying her ire
too much; it made her color rise and her hair fly
when she turned her head, and the faster breathing
made her perfect breasts go up and down in an
enticing rhythm. "What makes you so sure I'm a
greenhorn?" he asked mildly, still leaning on the
gate.

At last she looked straight at him, but she didn't
move from Butterpie's side. "Your hat, your boots—
that fancy red truck you drive. I'll bet it's custo-
mized."

Tanner grinned. Adjusted his hat. "Are you
telling me real cowboys don't drive red trucks?"

"There are lots of trucks around here," she

said. "Some of them are red, and some of them are new. And *all* of them are splattered with mud or manure or both."

"Maybe I ought to put in a car wash, then," he teased. "Sounds like there's a market for one. Might be a good investment."

She softened, though not significantly, and spared him a cautious half smile, full of questions she probably wouldn't ask. "There's a good car wash in Indian Rock," she informed him. "People go there. It's only forty miles."

"Oh," he said with just a hint of mockery. "*Only* forty miles. Well, then. Guess I'd better dirty up my truck if I want to be taken seriously in these here parts. Scuff up my boots a bit, too, and maybe stomp on my hat a couple of times."

Her cheeks went a fetching shade of pink. "You are twisting what I said," she told him, brushing Butterpie again, her touch gentle but sure. "I meant…"

Tanner envied that little horse. Wished he had a furry hide, so he'd need brushing, too.

"You *meant* that I'm not a real cowboy," he said. "And you could be right. I've spent a lot of time on construction sites over the last few years, or in meetings where a hat and boots wouldn't be appropriate. Instead of digging out my old gear, once I decided to take this job, I just bought new."

"I bet you don't even *have* any old gear," she

challenged, but she was smiling, albeit cautiously, as though she might withdraw into a disapproving frown at any second.

He took off his hat, extended it to her. "Here," he teased. "Rub that around in the muck until it suits you."

She laughed, and the sound—well, it caused a powerful and wholly unexpected shift inside him. Scared the hell out of him and, paradoxically, made him yearn to hear it again.

* * * * *

Discover how this rugged rancher's wanderlust
is tamed in time for a merry Christmas, in
A STONE CREEK CHRISTMAS.
In stores December 2008

HARLEQUIN® *Romance.*®

Marry-Me Christmas

by *USA TODAY* bestselling author

SHIRLEY JUMP

A *Bride* FOR ALL *Seasons*

Ruthless and successful journalist Flynn never mixes
business with pleasure. But when he's sent to write a
scathing review of Samantha's bakery, her beauty and
innocence catches him off guard. Has this small-town
girl unlocked the city slicker's heart?

Available December 2008.

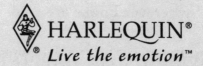

HARLEQUIN®
Live the emotion™

www.eHarlequin.com   HRI7557

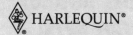
HARLEQUIN®

American ★ Romance®

HOLLY JACOBS
Once Upon a Christmas

Daniel McLean is thrilled to learn he
may be the father of Michelle Hamilton's
nephew. When Daniel starts to spend
time with Brandon and help her organize
Erie Elementary's big Christmas Fair, the
three discover a paternity test won't make
them a family, but the love they discover
just might....

*Available December 2008
wherever books are sold.*

LOVE, HOME & HAPPINESS

www.eHarlequin.com   HAR75242

REQUEST YOUR FREE BOOKS!

2 FREE NOVELS PLUS 2 FREE GIFTS!

HARLEQUIN®

Super Romance®

Exciting, emotional, unexpected!

YES! Please send me 2 FREE Harlequin Superromance® novels and my 2 FREE gifts (gifts are worth about $10). After receiving them, if I don't wish to receive any more books, I can return the shipping statement marked "cancel." If I don't cancel, I will receive 6 brand-new novels every month and be billed just $4.69 per book in the U.S. or $5.24 per book in Canada, plus 25¢ shipping and handling per book and applicable taxes, if any*. That's a savings of close to 15% off the cover price! I understand that accepting the 2 free books and gifts places me under no obligation to buy anything. I can always return a shipment and cancel at any time. Even if I never buy another book from Harlequin, the two free books and gifts are mine to keep forever.

135 HDN EEX7   336 HDN EEYK

Name	(PLEASE PRINT)	
Address		Apt. #
City	State/Prov.	Zip/Postal Code

Signature (if under 18, a parent or guardian must sign)

Mail to the **Harlequin Reader Service:**
IN U.S.A.: P.O. Box 1867, Buffalo, NY 14240-1867
IN CANADA: P.O. Box 609, Fort Erie, Ontario L2A 5X3

Not valid to current subscribers of Harlequin Superromance books.

Want to try two free books from another line?
Call 1-800-873-8635 or visit www.morefreebooks.com.

* Terms and prices subject to change without notice. N.Y. residents add applicable sales tax. Canadian residents will be charged applicable provincial taxes and GST. Offer not valid in Quebec. This offer is limited to one order per household. All orders subject to approval. Credit or debit balances in a customer's account(s) may be offset by any other outstanding balance owed by or to the customer. Please allow 4 to 6 weeks for delivery. Offer available while quantities last.

Your Privacy: Harlequin is committed to protecting your privacy. Our Privacy Policy is available online at www.eHarlequin.com or upon request from the Reader Service. From time to time we make our lists of customers available to reputable third parties who may have a product or service of interest to you. If you would prefer we not share your name and address, please check here. ☐

HSR08R

Harlequin® Historical
Historical Romantic Adventure!

THE MISTLETOE WAGER

Christine Merrill

Harry Pennyngton, Earl of Anneslea,
is surprised when his estranged wife,
Helena, arrives home for Christmas.
Especially when she's intent on
divorce! A festive house party
is in full swing when the guests
are snowed in, and Harry and
Helena find they are together
under the mistletoe....

Available December 2008
wherever books are sold.

#1530 A MAN TO RELY ON • Cindi Myers
Going Back
Scandal seems to follow Marisol Luna. And this trip home is no exception. She's not staying long in this town that can't forget who she was. Then she falls for Scott Redmond. Suddenly he's making her forget the gossip and rethink her exit plan.

#1531 NO PLACE LIKE HOME • Margaret Watson
The McInnes Triplets
All Bree McInnes has to do is make it through the summer without anyone discovering her secrets. But keeping a low profile turns out to be harder than the single mom thought—especially when her sexy professor-boss begins to fall in love. With her!

#1532 HIS ONLY DEFENSE • Carolyn McSparren
Count on a Cop
Cop rule number one: don't fall in love with a perp. Too bad Liz Gibson forgot that one. Except unlike everybody else, she doesn't believe Jud Slaughter killed his wife. Now she has to prove his innocence or lose him forever.

#1533 FOR THE SAKE OF THE CHILDREN • Cynthia Reese
You, Me & the Kids
Dana Wilson is *exactly* what Lissa thinks her single father needs. Dana is a single mom *and* the new school nurse. Lissa's dad, Patrick Connor, is chair of the board of education! Perfect? Well, there may be a few wrinkles that need ironing out....

#1534 THE SON BETWEEN THEM • Molly O'Keefe
A Little Secret
Samantha Riggins keeps pulling J. D. Kronos back. With her he is a better man and can forget his P.I. world. But when he discovers the secret she's been hiding, nothing is the same. And now J.D. must choose between his former life and a new one with Samantha.

#1535 MEANT FOR EACH OTHER • Lee Duran
Everlasting Love
Since the moment they met, Frankie has loved Johnny Davis. Yet their love hasn't always been enough to make things work. Then Johnny is injured and needs her. As she rushes to his side, Frankie discovers the true value of being meant for each other.